D0679101

Left Behind in Squabble Bay

Left Behind in Squabble Bay

by
Jack Hodgins

Illustrated by VictoR GAD

M&S

Canadian Cataloguing in Publication Data
Hodgins, Jack, 1938-
    Left behind in Squabble Bay

ISBN 0-7710-4191-8

I. GAD, VictoR. II. Title.

PS8565.03L43 1988   jC813'.54   C88-093538-3
PZ7.H63Le 1988

Design and typesetting by VictoR GAD studio
Printed and bound in Canada by Friesen Printers

McClelland and Stewart
The Canadian Publishers
481 University Avenue
Toronto, Ontario
M5G 2E9

for Tyler

Chapter One

Nearly every day at this time, late in the afternoon, Alex McGuire could be seen on the beach below town. Sometimes he walked with his head down, kicking at the debris left behind by the tide. Often he stood at the water's edge and tossed one pebble after another, as though he intended to throw the entire gravel beach into the sea. Occasionally he collected shells for Frantic Freda, who sat out at the end of the wharf under her yellow umbrella, making seashell jewelry that nobody ever wanted.

Though the front of his peaked cap said SMILE, the look on the face beneath it was far from happy. As everyone knew, this long-legged skinny kid was not at all pleased to be here. He hadn't wanted to come to this place; he hadn't wanted to stay. His father had brought him here one day and simply *left* him. He considered himself a prisoner now, with no real hope of escape.

And what a place to be a prisoner – Squabble Bay! This was a little pulp mill town surrounded by rainy mountains and dark-green forest – far from anywhere else. This was a town where no one ever listened to anyone else, where no one ever spoke a civil word if it could be avoided. Nobody ever seemed to laugh here. Nobody smiled. The rule seemed to be, "If you can't say something nasty about your neighbour, then at least you should try to ignore him." Anyone looking out a window and seeing him now would say, "There's that kid from Back East. Why doesn't he find some *normal* friends his own age instead of hanging around with that crazy old bat on the wharf?"

Today, when he'd walked out the length of the wharf to deliver a coffee can half full of shells for her jewelry, Frantic Freda stirred a finger around inside and leaned close to look them over, her long crooked nose nearly inside the can. "Nothing too wonderful in here," she said.

"I picked the best I could find."

She sniffed. "Well, at least you didn't throw in bits of crab legs and seaweed this time. I just may get you beach-trained after all, though it hasn't been easy." But then suddenly she threw back her head, sniffed hard at the air, and cried out, "I smell trouble!"

Alex smelled nothing in the air himself. But when Frantic Freda had climbed the rickety ladder down the side of the wharf, she stuck her finger into the sea water and licked it. Then she squinted up her little eyes and said, "Oboy, there's a whopper coming! Watch out, the world's about to get a shaking up!"

But Frantic Freda was always making crazy predictions based on the smell of the air or the taste of the sea or the peculiar shape of a passing cloud, and nobody paid much attention. Now, as her frizzy mop of electric grey hair rose back up the ladder, she turned to look in at the town, and frowned in the direction of the little flat-roofed corner store that overlooked the beach – owned by Alex's aunt. What did she see? Suddenly she puffed up and trembled all over. "Stop him!" she shouted. The huge yellow gumboots on the end of her

skinny legs did a quick impatient dance on the planks. "Stop that man!"

Stop what man? Alex saw someone standing outside the store. Did he have a gun? What if it was an escaped killer? What if it was a wild man who had come down out of those mountains, someone who'd gone crazy-in-the-head from living alone, someone who wanted a captive to feed to his pet cougar? That was the kind of thought that came to Alex. What if the worst thing you could imagine should come true?

Freda didn't seem to worry about such things. She hurried up the pebbly slope of the beach, her yellow-striped raincoat flapping around her bony knees – thumped and panted in her big rubber boots up the shaky wooden steps that climbed the bank. Alex followed, though not too close behind.

"Take off!" she shouted, waving her arms about. "Nobody asked you back! Nobody wants you back! Just go away!"

She was yelling at someone he had never seen before. A large, big-bellied man in overalls. He was bald on the front half of his skull, but a wild bush of red hair flew up from the back half like the feathery tail of an ostrich. Tiny eyes blinked. He had one huge hand wrapped around the store's door handle, but he hadn't opened the door yet. Instead, he seemed to be backing away from Freda. "I just wanted to get me some food. I'm running a little short."

Surely a stranger had the right to walk into a store without being yelled at. "He can go in," Alex said. "My aunt's inside – she owns it."

Frantic Freda snapped her fingers – dry as old bones. "Away! Away!" She acted as if she were a magician trying to make the stranger disappear.

The stranger looked embarrassed. Maybe being yelled at was more upsetting when a boy was watching. Alex wished he had stayed down on the beach. Something was happening here that he didn't understand. He tried to put a "keep-me-out-of-this" look on his face, but he knew he appeared awkward and curious.

Maybe Freda had good reason for trying to chase the big man away. What if he'd robbed this store at one time – bopped Aunt on the head with a bag of onions and took money from the till? He must be seven feet tall and strong enough to bash down that door. He looked as if he could take hold of the store by one corner and lift it off its foundation and give it a good shake to scare Aunt into giving him anything he wanted.

Not that Alex could imagine anyone brave enough to threaten his aunt. One look would be enough to scare off most savages, cut-throats and desperadoes. He'd seen loggers tremble at just a few words from her razor tongue.

Here she was now, opening her door, poking her broad angry face into the world. "What's going on? What's all this racket?" She held her broom like a long-barrelled gun. The aluminum safety hat – which she wore when she helped Uncle down on the log booms but never took off even when she was in the store – made Alex think of an old-time soldier's helmet.

Then she saw the stranger. "You! Where did you come from? Who asked you back?"

Was she going to hit him with the broom? In an animated cartoon she would. Short thick Aunt would raise it and bring it down so hard on his head her own feet would leave the floor. A goose egg would swell up immediately on his scalp and shine like a lighthouse beacon. He would hear birds singing and see stars and –

But this wasn't an animated cartoon. If she bopped this man on the head with her broom, he was big enough to pick her up and toss her into the sea. Alex half hoped this would happen. Aunt in her hard hat shooting out like a rocket to splash down amongst seals and sockeye salmon – that would be something to see!

Instead, the stranger acted like an uncomfortable clown, whirling his finger at his own temple. "You know how absent-minded I've always been. Completely forgot to stock up. Cupboard's almost bare."

You couldn't imagine Aunt smiling even at a real clown. "Go stock up somewhere else. Ya musta been going *somewhere* all these years! I thought you had better sense than to come back here."

"Just thought enough time had gone by – "

Aunt looked as if she'd like to poke the broom handle into his stomach. "Go rummage in the dump. You'll never see the inside of my store again." She stepped inside and pulled the door closed with a bang.

Alex felt awful. What was it like to be treated this way? The man must feel like crying – though of course he couldn't, being an adult. Not here at least.

Instead, he seemed to sag, as if someone had pulled his skeleton right out of him through the bottom of his feet. His head drooped, his great shoulders slumped, his back curved. Then, looking at Alex with an awkward and sad expression, he shrugged and stepped down off the porch and started away.

"Wait!" Alex hadn't intended to say anything. The word just came out. He ran to catch up to the man, who turned and looked at him.

He wanted to say: I'm not surprised at the way they treated you. You should see the way they treat me!

He wanted to say: What did you do? Did you hurt somebody?

Instead, lowering his voice so that Frantic Freda couldn't hear from the front of the store, he said, "There's milk and food and stuff in my aunt's kitchen."

The man placed a hand on his bald scalp and looked confused. "Yes, I imagine there is. And it looks as though she'd fight to the death to keep it there."

"But I mean – " What did he mean? "I mean – if you want me to get you some – " Was that really what he'd meant, that he would *smuggle,* when he didn't even know this man?

The man seemed to be thinking something similar. He looked as though he were about to say: Who are you to be offering food out of your aunt's fridge to a total stranger? But eventually he almost smiled. "You'd take a chance of making *her* mad at you?"

Alex looked back at his aunt's store, where her broad angry face was watching him through the window. She gave the broom a threatening shake. "But – " he said. "What I meant was – "

"That's okay," the man said. He put a hand on the top of Alex's cap. "I guess any milk in her fridge would be sour anyway. Besides, it isn't milk I want. I need a new paint brush. Some popcorn. A few cans of soup. She got those in her fridge?" Then he turned, stepped across the weedy ditch, and disappeared into the thick underbrush beneath the stand of firs.

What if he really was hungry? What if he was starving, and only pretending not to be?

What if he had no home? No place to go? What if he had to live with the wolves?

There. It had started again – worrying. Alex knew what he was – a worrywart. Not just an ordinary worrywart. Not just the I-hope-I-don't-flunk-this-test kind of worrywart. Not just the I-hope-things-don't-turn-out-to-be-as-bad-as-I-know-they-are-going-to-be kind of occasional worrywart. He was the kind of worrywart who began every sentence, practically every thought, with "What if?"

"What if all this dumb rain rusts the braces on my teeth?" "What if the tide comes in too far by mistake and forgets to go out?" "What if a foreign spy sneaks in here at night and takes us all hostage?" "What if nobody pays the ransom?"

That kind of worrywart.

No use telling him to stop worrying. People had tried. His own father had told him when he was very small that worrywarts turn into wart hogs, but it only gave him something new to worry about. What if he turned into a wart hog and a farmer mistook him for a runaway pig? Could he live his life in a pen?

Oh, it was amazing how many things Alex McGuire could find to worry about. "What if Billie Tonelli's spit wads knock Miss MacAdam's red wig off in the middle of an arithmetic lesson and she thinks it was me and locks me in a closet for a year?" "What if someone sneaks into the house to steal the television set and gets fingerprints on my collections of X-men comics?" "What if it's really true what they say about this place, that it hardly ever snows here for Christmas?" After all, there were only a few days left before Christmas and the weather had hardly changed since he'd arrived a month ago – just rain and the threat of more rain. "What if this soggy climate starts moss growing on my nose?"

"What if that man really is hungry?" he asked his aunt, once he'd stepped inside her store. Freda had gone back out to the wharf, to her seashell jewelry.

"Let him be hungry! Did you come in here to buy something or just to wear out my ears?"

"But – "

"*But but,*" she mimicked, twisting her mouth out of shape. She was up on a ladder counting cans of tomatoes on a shelf.

"But what did he do that was so terrible?"

"Never mind. Something you're too young to understand."

"But – "

"*But but.* Here comes that motorboat again!"

He couldn't help it. Questions just came. What if, what if, what if? "What if every store turns the man away?"

"Tough!"

"What if his feelings were hurt?"

"I hope they were! That's the whole idea – keep him away!"

But what if he's got a kid somewhere? What if he's got a whole bunch of crying kids and nothing to eat in the house?

"He used to live here," his aunt said, stepping down off the ladder. "But we don't want him around anymore. Now, are you going to pay me for that can of pop or not? The till won't take worrywart questions for money."

Alex put the can of pop back inside the cooler. "I guess I don't feel like buying anything."

"And stay away from that crazy Freda too," his aunt said.

What? Freda was the only person in this place who didn't get cranky with him. "I *help* her."

"Helping a lunatic is nothing to brag about."

"She *likes* me!"

"She's crazy. Try making friends with some *normal* people for a change."

"Like who? Who's normal around here?"

"Watch that tongue of yours, mister! Go on outside – find some kids to play with. Get!"

Alex didn't feel like staying here any longer. He didn't even feel very bad when he slammed the door so hard the OPEN sign fell off its hook. He kicked the bottom railing of the porch. What kind of person would chase away a man who might have hungry children depending on him for their next meal? Even if he was supposed to have done something terrible. If he'd escaped from prison, maybe it was because they had put him in by mistake. If he'd robbed this store once, maybe it was so those kids wouldn't starve.

Anyone looking out a window could see the kid from Back East was brooding. He yanked down his SMILE cap to hide his eyes but it was still obvious that his face was pulled into a terrible scowl as he walked along the beach on his long skinny legs, his thin shoulders hunched forward like a question mark. When he was in a good mood, he took great long strides and put a sort of spring into every step – Old-step-and-a-half, his dad had sometimes called him. But when he was glum, as he was now, he walked as if his shoes were filled with rocks.

After a while he chose twenty small flat stones and skipped them over the waves. One after the other he side-armed them out and watched them hop across the water until they sank. Some sank right away; some went glancing off wave after wave. A pale-green one touched the surface eighteen times before sinking – double his own record.

Now skipping twenty pebbles should be enough to

work out most of the bad feeling after an incident like the one at the store. But Alex was worrying about other things as well. He went into his aunt and uncle's house – a long trailer attached to the flat-roofed little store – and got his white drafting board with the green grid lines on it, his long black technical pen, and his largest pad of paper. Then he went down the beach to sit in the shelter of some driftwood planks he'd wedged between two logs. The rain had stopped, but he'd been here long enough to know it was only taking a break.

What would he draw? He didn't know. Something that showed how badly he wanted to get out of here. Something that showed how mad he was at his father for dumping him in Squabble Bay while *he* went off to have adventures in the world. Exploring rivers. Living with jungle tribes. Discovering ancient treasures.

Deserter!

The trouble was that for years Alex had led a fairly normal and happy life with his father back in Ottawa. They'd lived in a narrow brick house overlooking the canal, and because his father was what he called a Single Parent with a Double Responsibility, he made sure there was always something for them to do together. They skated. They skied. In spring they drove into the country where they stopped to watch a farmer making maple syrup from the sap he drained from the trees. In fall they took a boat trip up the canal system to stop and listen to stories told by the old-timers staying in cottages along the banks.

Then one day they drove out into the Valley to attend a cattle auction where they saw a panicked calf jump over the fence of the show ring and land on top of a woman sitting in the front row of the bleachers. Driving home, Alex's father said he knew how that poor woman felt. He had an announcement to make. His new bosses had decided, he said, to send him off to live in some jungle village in South America for a couple of years.

Alex could see that his father wasn't really as disappointed by this news as he pretended to be. He even seemed excited about it. "But the trouble is," he explained, "they're sending me where a person would be crazy to take a kid."

"Even if the kid wanted to go along?"

"Even if the kid *begged!*"

"Even if the kid promised to behave? And swore he would never complain about snakes or cannibals or anything?"

There was no point in arguing. Alex was not allowed to go, even if it meant he would be uprooted from his home and dragged right across this continent – halfway to Japan! – then left in Squabble Bay, in this unfriendly place on the west coast where his father had grown up long ago, to live with the grouchiest aunt and uncle in the world.

And not a friend in sight. The only real friends he'd ever had still lived in what people here called "Back East." Going to school had got him some classmates. Learning how to play soccer in their muddy field had got him some team-mates. But classmates and team-mates weren't automatically your friends. After a month of living here he still hadn't met a single comic book collector like himself. What if he never did? What if there wasn't a person living on this coast who knew Cyclops from Superman? What if there wasn't anyone here who cared what happened to Wolverine? Back home his best friend Mark had a collection even larger than his own. Every day after school or basketball practice the two of them would get together and talk about their heroes. They had even started a series of their own. Mark made up the stories; Alex drew them. The hero was The Blade, who could save the entire population of a big city from the sticky fingers of Golop the Gluey Monster. Now Alex was drawing The Blade alone.

Too bad The Blade wasn't real! With his X-ray eyes he could search every house on this island until he spotted someone with a secret collection of X-men comics – a possible friend. With his super powers he could fill this bay with snow, freeze up the rivers, even turn the ocean into a giant skating rink – give them a real winter. Or better still, he could just transfer Alex back to Mark's house and prevent the authorities from ever finding him.

By the time he'd finished the drawing, the tide had come up the slope of the gravel beach as far as his feet. Waves lapped at his runners. It was nearly dark. Freda had left the wharf. The lights were on in the rusty old boat she lived in, out at the end of the breakwater. Soon he wouldn't be able to see what he'd drawn.

In fact, what he had drawn wasn't too bad. A great crowded cartoon. Mark would like it.

But Mark would also tell him to burn it fast. What if someone in Squabble Bay should see it?

The whole neighbourhood was on the page. All the houses clustered around the bay had become ugly, dilapidated shacks, a shanty town, a slum – surrounded by a herd of thick hairy beasts, each with the scowling face of someone who lived here. There was Miss MacAdam. There was the garage mechanic's big nose. There were Jake and Felicity and Billie Tonelli – some of the kids from school – stretched out, grotesque, with distorted hostile faces. Anyone could see that he thought living here was about as much fun as sticking your face into a heap of rotting starfish.

"Hey, what're you doin'?"

Felicity Bogg, a girl from school, was sauntering this way with her hands inside the bib of her blue-jean overalls. She sounded as if she was sure he was doing something stupid and filthy.

"Nothing." He turned the picture away but she moved closer.

"Who are those people?" Her finger jabbed at the paper. "Who's this?" Her freckled nose wrinkled up. Her wide blue eyes accused him of something horrible.

She was the kind of girl who grinned scornfully at you in school without saying anything so that you would wonder if there was toothpaste on your nose. If you let your hand do what it just had to do – check the zipper on your fly – she laughed out loud. Think how she'd laugh if he ran away!

"Who is it?" She sucked on the end of a handful of her own long pale hair.

"Nobody." He tried to close the sketch pad but she held it open with a firm grip.

"Oh sure! The page is blank and I'm imagining things!"

"Nobody *real,* I meant."

"Who's this? It's Miss MacAdam. Oboy. And this. It's *Billie!*"

"Sort of," he said. Well, it wasn't really Billie Tonelli. It was sort of how he *felt* about him.

He tried again to close up the pad but Felicity pushed his hand back. "And this?" she said. "This is *me!*"

Anybody could have seen that. Those big crooked protruding front teeth were unmistakable – far worse than his own had been before they stuck these braces in.

"You sewer sandwich! That's *me!*"

"But – "

"Who do you think you are, drawing *me?* Give me that!"

She grabbed at the sketch pad but he held on. "No! I was just going to tear it up." He pulled. "Let go."

"They're gonna put you in chains when they see this, brace-face," she said. She tugged at the paper again. "They'll lock you up in the yard like a dog that chases chickens. There's your *aunt! I recognize your aunt. Give me that!!!!*"

He held tight. Even a torn-off fragment would be enough to condemn him.

"Wait till your aunt sees this, she'll feed you to the seals!"

"But – but – what if I draw you a picture of your own? What if I draw you some trees? Killer whales!"

She crossed her eyes and stuck her finger down her throat to show what she thought of killer whales.

"What if I draw you again then? What if I draw you right?"

"And what if I show this around, you eastern city snot! What if people see what you think of us!"

Felicity Bogg yanked the sketch pad out of his grasp.

Tore out the page.

Tossed the pad back at him.

If he threw himself at her now, knocked her down, grabbed the paper, tore it to shreds –

He tried. Imagined a football tackle, and charged. But he was awkard and sprawling – no football player. When he tried to grab her legs she quickly stepped aside, leapt onto a log. He fell. A thousand tiny stones imbedded themselves in his open palms.

"You want it back that bad?"

She held the page behind her and danced on her toes.

"But it isn't yours," he said. "What – what if – what if I tell them you stole?"

"*You stole.*" She mimicked him. "I'll give it back if you – " She thought about it. "If you do all my math homework for a month."

He wasn't too bad at math. But *could* he?

"And draw a picture that makes me look like a movie star. And sign your name on it so everyone can see that you think I'm beautiful."

He sat on the damp gravel, pulled his knees right up under his chin and wrapped his arms around them. Felicity Bogg, beautiful? He made a face.

"And if you take off one of your big stinky sneakers and fill it with sea water and *drink* it!"

He was ashamed that he'd thought about bargaining with her.

"Go ahead and keep it then." His voice was shaking and cracking. "If you want everyone to see you took something that isn't yours."

"Oh, I'm so worried! Tin-grin!"

She jumped off the log and hurried away, gravel spraying out behind each heel. "Just wait'll your aunt and uncle get their hands on you, metal-mouth – your life is over!" She skipped away down the beach, waving his big piece of paper around in the air like a captured flag.

Now what was he going to do? He couldn't go home. Not now. He couldn't stay here either. His behind was already wet and itchy from sitting on the gravel. He'd have to spend the night somewhere else. In Freda's sunken warship out at the end of the breakwater? She'd be in bed already; she'd even be asleep. She snoozed off soon after the sky began to darken and didn't like being disturbed. "If I don't get lots of sleep," she once told Alex, "I'll lose my special powers for reading the signs."

He would have to hide in somebody's shed along the beach. What if he went to the Duchess-in-exile's shed? What if he snuck into her old tilted boat house and closed the door behind him? No one would know. The tall old Duchess-in-exile with all her glittering jewels hardly ever went into it; she'd never find him. He wished he could stay there until his father returned, but that could take years, and he would have nothing to eat. He would stay there just until he thought of some way to get himself out of this mess – or until some superhero like The Blade came roaring in to his rescue.

Chapter Two

When he awoke in the dark, he could hear Uncle's gruff voice calling him from up by the store. Then Uncle's voice was joined by others, from every direction. How long had they been calling? Running footsteps thumped past. Someone hollered: "Call the police! Check your basements. Look in your doghouse. We'll go through these sheds!"

Within moments three men came in through the door and shone flashlights in his face. "C'm'ere, you!" someone barked. Piston-rod Joe, a mechanic with the logging company, wrapped a large rough hand around Alex's arm and hauled him up onto his feet. "Tell them we found their brat."

Piston-rod and another man held his upper arms in a tight grip and escorted him up off the beach to the door of the trailer. Within moments Alex could see that he was in trouble. The guilty cartoon was mounted on the kitchen wall, soiled and wrinkled from passing through dozens of angry hands. Like a criminal hung up by his thumbs. Before these two were through with him, would they have him hanging beside it?

Aunt sucked in her breath. She closed her weaker eye and let the other one bulge as she leaned close to him. "Maybe you think it's all right to make fun of people.

26

Did your father teach you to be *mean?"* She was so mad she was trembling. Maybe she would explode.

Her hands, which were nearly as rough and stubby as Uncle's, with black dirt beneath the broken nails, reminded him of the front claws of the tyrannosaurus rex in the National Museum.

"But my father told me – " he began. He could not control his shaky voice. "What if – what if – ? He said it never hurt to let people know how you feel."

Uncle slurped his cocoa, then wiped his sleeve across his beard. "Your old man's head's in the clouds," he said. "That's the kind of garbage they teach at university."

"But he said if people learned to laugh at themselves, they wouldn't – "

"Haw." The sound came right up from the bottom of Uncle's stomach. "If he'd stayed here and worked around normal people he might've got different ideas."

"Careful," Aunt muttered, gritting her teeth. "This is his father you're talking about."

Uncle looked as though he wanted to growl. "Well, he's sure as blazes not bein' much of a father right now, is he? He dumped the job on somebody else."

Aunt jabbed the end of a finger at the drawing on the wall. "The point is, Alex – are you paying attention? Do you really think there's anything to laugh at in this?" She pulled out a chair and motioned him to sit at the table while she made him a cup of cocoa. "Do you think Mrs. Blimmer should laugh at the mosquito head you gave her? Don't worry, I can tell who most of these are. Poor woman, I don't know how I'll face her again."

"But – "

"But but! Just look what you did to Mr. Klinck! He'll never forgive us!" She poured water out of the kettle

into his cup. "Maybe you think your uncle should be laughing because you gave him the face of an idiot cave man?"

Would he be punished for this? Aunt never got tired of saying that she didn't believe in punishment. Once in a dentist's waiting room she'd read a magazine article that told her it was better to rely on something called Natural Consequences.

The first time he'd wandered too far and been late getting home, the Natural Consequences had been: "Too bad you weren't here. We drove downtown to that science fiction movie you wanted to see. It was wonderful!"

The second time he was late, he found all his belongings sitting out on the sidewalk. "We thought you'd gone for good," his aunt said. "We'd almost rented your room to a boarder who would appreciate it."

What was the Natural Consequences for drawing a picture that made an entire neighbourhood look like a herd of unfriendly beasts? Uncle would probably like to beat him up, but Aunt would never let that happen. A beating would make *everyone* miserable. The purpose of Natural Consequences, as far as Alex could tell, was to make sure that Alex was the only one who suffered.

Uncle peered first at the scandalous picture on the wall, then at the criminal who'd drawn it. "When I was a kid I made fun of someone once, so my old man he got me a job in a coal mine," he said. "That cured me fast."

Fish scales flew out from the hairs of his hand. He hardly ever washed. Scales winked like flakes of red and blue glass in the tangled hair of his beard.

"Now that's not quite true," Aunt said. "Your father took you down a mine shaft to show you what life was like for people without an education. You've

never been down one since."

"He did not," Uncle said. "What do you know about it anyway?"

"Oh, but he did," Aunt said. "Please stop and think before you're so sure of things."

"Who was there at the time – you or me?"

"I've heard you tell about this before and it was quite a different story then. But maybe I'm too stupid to remember it right. Maybe I should just put myself in an institution for the feeble-minded."

Whenever his aunt and uncle started arguing like this, Alex found himself sliding down on his seat until he was able to slip under the table and wait for them to finish. When grownups started acting like kids, you didn't want to see anything higher than knees. To Alex they seemed to behave like cartoon characters.

Gruff and Grump were the names he gave them. She's Gruff, he's Grump. From the rear they look like two identical thick dark stumps. From the front they look much the same, except they have two broad grouchy faces with tiny dark eyes like the shells of insects. They both wear smelly boots, thick woollen pants, and dark plaid mackinaws – even in the house. And of course their hard hats.

"Did so!"

"Did not!"

"Did so!"

Uncle lifts both feet in the air and brings them down on the floor. "You're a stubborn old miserable *baboon!*"

"And you," Aunt Gruff yells, "are a bone-headed goat-smelling *turkey!*"

"A stubborn old miserable cross-eyed alligator-faced baboon!"

Aunt Gruff picks up a mug and turns it over to let

cocoa slop onto Uncle's head. Cocoa ran into one eye.

Of course the real Aunt and Uncle never went quite so far as to turn over cocoa cups on their heads. "Now that we've got 'the boy' living with us," Aunt liked to say, "we have to set a good example." To set a good example they seldom resorted to violence; they mostly just shouted at one another.

"Well," said Uncle, "it don't matter if my old man sent me down a coal mine or not. The point is – *now you get up from under there!*"

Alex climbed out from beneath the table and decided it was just about time to go to bed, even if he hadn't had any supper and his stomach was complaining that a cup of cocoa was not enough. They could yell some more at breakfast if they wanted to but right now he just wanted to be alone. "Excuse me," he said, and headed for his bedroom.

Uncle followed and prevented Alex from closing the door. "The point is," he said, "you can't come to a place like this, eh, and eat off your relatives, and then turn around and spit in the neighbours' faces."

"I don't imagine he'll ever do it again," Aunt said, coming up behind.

"He'll do it again if he gets the chance," Uncle said. "He can keep himself outa trouble by helping at work." He paused to let this sink in.

"But – but isn't it a holiday?"

"*We'll* keep you busy enough. Starting tomorrow morning."

Alex looked at his aunt. He was sure he hadn't been told about this before. For him Christmas holidays had always been a time for travel – into the Gatineau Hills maybe, to do some skiing. The least he had hoped for here was to be left alone.

"It's what your father would want," Aunt said.

Uncle worked amongst the logs before they went up the conveyor belt and into the Mill to be ground up into pulp for making paper. Alex had watched him once. Out in the water – the "salt chuck," as Uncle called it – he herded the floating logs much as cowboys herd cattle, gathering them and starting them on their way up that chute. He wore caulk boots and walked on the floating logs, which dipped and bobbed beneath his weight, and carried a long pointed pole for the purpose of pushing them around. Was he going to make Alex do *that?*

Aunt operated a dozer boat, a little round tub that she could steer in any direction, with a jagged iron set of teeth down the point of the prow for pushing the logs ahead of her once Uncle had got them unjammed.

For someone who had never been near the sea before, it seemed a dangerous place to work. If they had their way, he wouldn't live to see the New Year.

"Do I have to? What if I fall in and drown?"

"And don't complain about it either," Uncle said.

"We're not even going to bring up the fact that you worried us half to death," Aunt said, "thinking you had been kidnapped or killed or got yourself lost in the woods. I can't even imagine how fierce a punishment such a thing would deserve. If we believed in punishment."

The moment he'd turned out the light and crawled into bed, Aunt tapped on the door and opened it wide enough for the hall light to shine on his face. "We'll just bundle up all your drawing things in the morning," she said. "All those pens and paper and that awkward board that got you into this trouble. We'll find a garage sale and get some money for them!"

He sat up in bed, not believing his ears. "But you can't – "

"Now don't be selfish," she warned. "Since you're not going to use them anymore yourself, why shouldn't someone else get pleasure out of them? A little kid who isn't healthy or strong enough to do anything useful."

They would have to tie him up or lock him in a closet before they took away his pens or his drawing board. He thought of booby traps and guard dogs. He hoped a pair of tough ex-convicts would wander into town and say they were looking for work as hired gunmen.

"Let the kid sleep," Uncle called from down the hall. "We've gotta get up in the morning. This is a working man's family. He's gonna get a taste of what it means to earn a living."

Aunt started to close the door, then stopped. "After work tomorrow you'll go out and apologize to the neighbours. Try to save this family's reputation."

He let his head smack into the pillow.

"Your aunt and uncle aren't *trying* to be mean," Alex's dad had told him when he first complained about having to stay here. "They just don't have any experience."

"You want them to practise on me?"

There was no way Alex was going to let them get rid of his drawing equipment. "I'll hide it," he said into the dark room.

He waited until his aunt and uncle were asleep, snoring like two saws working their way through separate logs. Then he found a flashlight, pulled his clothes on over his pajamas, and began the job of moving his art supplies out to safety. With most of his equipment stuffed into his backpack and his drawing board under one arm, he snuck out the back door of the house, down the steps to the gravel, along the chilly beach past the slapping waves, and into the Duchess-in-exile's boat house, where he'd hidden earlier tonight.

There was no boat in the Duchess-in-exile's boat house; only a collection of rusty motors, chairs with broken legs, stacks of lumber, boxes of bottles, ancient suitcases, and some heavy travelling trunks. He stacked all the china to one end of the purple trunk with stickers from Panama and India on the top, and made room for his art supplies.

Closing the lid, he realized that his comic book collection was still in as much danger back in his bedroom as his art equipment had been. He imagined Aunt and Uncle deciding to turn all the X-men and Cerebus the Aardvarks over to a yard sale where someone would charge only ten cents each. Kids would throw away their plastic envelopes, read them once (with food on their fingers!) and toss them into the garbage. Toss Cerebus into the garbage! Teachers would rip them out of hands at school. Someone would fill in all the mail-away coupons just for the pleasure of printing words on that soft paper. Felicity Bogg would doodle in the margins with a pen. Billie Tonelli would tear the pages into strips and chew them up into spit wads. Chew up X-men! Chew up Superman! What if the entire collection were chewed up into spit wads for a gigantic playground war?

The comic book collection would have to be hidden too.

Two boxes at a time – one under each arm – he made three trips to move his comics out of the house and into the boat shed. He removed strange-smelling stacks of cloth from the black trunk and stored them in the empty interior of an old clothes dryer. He removed shoe boxes of photographs and cartons of silver cutlery and baskets of unfinished knitting from the blue trunk and stuffed them in the old icebox. Then all of the comics could fit.

And yet he didn't feel like going back to Aunt and Uncle's house. He felt like drawing. Before he left his equipment here, he would pencil in another page of The Blade. Why not? He could mail it to Mark. He propped the flashlight on top of the icebox and let it shine down. The striped legs of his pajamas showed below the jeans he'd pulled on over them. He wore no socks inside his runners; his ankles were shiny and pale in this light.

In the first panel he showed The Blade capturing a criminal in a dark alley of a big city. In the second panel The Blade discovered that his friend needed help. How did he know this? The Blade put such importance on friendship that a friend's plea for help was something he could pick up even across a continent.

How could he knock on people's doors and say that he was sorry? What if Miss MacAdam slammed the door in his face? What if Felicity's parents chased him out into the bush to starve, like the big man in overalls, and then a bunch of hunters started shooting at him?

What if the hunters put a bullet through one of his legs and took him away to some foreign country and made him beg on the streets?

What if his own father came down the street and hollered, "Get away from me, you filthy beggar, I've never seen you before!"

Suddenly an electric light came on – a bare bulb hanging from the rafters. Alex jumped. An angry voice cried out behind him, "What are you doing in here?"

The Duchess-in-exile stood in the doorway in a long green robe. She may have been the tallest woman in Squabble Bay. Certainly she was the thinnest. She went

35

up and up, as if she were a long narrow stem, with the small pale flower of her face blooming at the top. A band of coloured jewels glittered in her heap of grey hair. Huge flashing earrings dangled from her ears. Several necklaces of different colours and sizes winked at her throat. Around the back of her neck a long white cat lay draped, its tail hanging down over one shoulder and its head nestling between its paws on the other. Jewels sparkled in its collar.

Two pairs of green eyes glared at Alex.

"I thought we had evicted you once already tonight," said the Duchess-in-exile. She spoke, of course, with a British accent.

"But – "

She lowered her great heavy painted blue eyelids and peered down at him suspiciously, her hand pressed to the necklaces at her throat. "How do I know you aren't a thief?" A ring shone on every finger.

Alex held his drawing board against his chest like a shield. "I wouldn't take anything of yours." His voice sounded like someone else's.

The blue eyelids slid up and her gaze shifted about the room. "How do I know you aren't an assassin sent by the Royal Family – to dispose of me and steal all my precious belongings?" The cat stared at Alex. "Fortunately, I wear my jewelry to bed."

"But I . . . I . . . don't have any weapons." He spread his arms wide to show how innocent he was.

"Don't be alarmed," she said, her voice softening. "I must put on a show of sounding fierce occasionally – for Mrs. Digby-Smith here." On her shoulder Mrs. Digby-Smith yawned and seemed to grin at Alex. One ear twitched. Did the cat know what was being said? "In the old days we could make lords and ladies quiver just by raising an eyebrow."

"I didn't want to stay here," Alex said. "I only wanted to hide my comic collection – from my uncle and aunt."

"Ahhhhhhhh!" The long green stem leaned to one side, then righted itself and moved a few steps closer. "They hid whole libraries in caves during the war. To keep civilization alive." She leaned forward to stare into his face. "Perhaps that's what you're doing?"

"And my equipment."

She looked hard at Alex while she made a decision. "Well, I suppose Mrs. Digby-Smith and I will stand guard over your treasures." Flinging herself upright, she turned and opened the blue trunk and seemed to be reading the titles on the comics.

"I saw them chasing this man away – "

"I know, I know. Poor fellow. What did you do with my silver?"

"In the icebox."

"Of course." She opened the icebox and saw that he'd told her the truth.

Since she seemed harmless enough, she might be willing to explain a few things. "They wouldn't tell me why they chased that man away. What if he's got a whole bunch of hungry kids?"

She closed the icebox door with a thunk. "They'd be ashamed to tell you. Or ought to be."

"Do you know him?"

The Duchess-in-exile turned her head to look directly into the eyes of Mrs. Digby-Smith, as though she were expecting to find an answer there. When the cat hoisted its shoulders in a sort of shrug and looked away, the Duchess-in-exile turned to Alex again. "I suppose I knew him once."

"Does he have starving children do you think? Or –

what if he's an escaped criminal?"

She closed her great blue eyelids and shook her head. "Not a criminal."

"And the children?"

"Good heavens! Am I on trial here? It was years ago that I saw him last."

"What if he doesn't have a place to live?"

She spoke now as though she were speaking to herself. "As a young man he used to find me amusing – an old blue-blood exiled to the edge of the world. He wanted to know if I had been a criminal in the Old Country, to be banished here. 'You must have done something pretty terrible to deserve *this!*' He'd have me in stitches while he guessed what crimes I'd committed. Putting snakes in the Queen's bed! Spilling the Duke's cup of tea!"

Why *was* she exiled here, he wanted to ask. Was she really a Duchess? Had she left a castle behind? But if he started asking questions like that, he would never find out about the stranger who had been thrown out of town. "Nobody's told me his name."

Her eyes sparkled like her jewels, as though he'd invited her to play a game. "His name? Well – *ouch!*"

The cat had raised a paw and, hooking a claw on the large earring, given it a tug. The Duchess-in-exile looked alarmed. "Oh, for goodness sake! What harm would there be?" Her great blue-lidded eyes looked down on Alex with some uncertainty. "Well, then – let's just say you'd be surprised. You may even have seen his picture in the papers."

Mrs. Digby-Smith tugged at the earring again, then rose as though she would leap off the shoulder and abandon a human partner who didn't know when to stop telling too much.

The Duchess-in-exile looked confused but placed a hand on the cat's back to keep her in place. "You're from Back East. They have a different idea of what makes a celebrity there. Don't they, Mrs. D?"

The cat, apparently satisfied, settled again on the woman's shoulder and rubbed her nose against the bejewelled neck. The Duchess-in-exile's hand stroked her repeatedly. "If you're thinking of running for mayor so you can change things around here, forget it. I tried that myself. It didn't work. Three people voted for me and two of them spoiled their ballots by writing nasty things on them."

"But – "

"You could buy space in the weekly Press. Hire one of those planes that drag signs behind them – list your complaints. See if anyone cares. I wouldn't count on it."

"But I – "

"What I don't understand," she said, "is why you're so unimaginative about where you hide. The first time *I* ran away from home I didn't stop until I reached the Himalayas. I wouldn't have stopped even then if one of my father's servants hadn't been waiting for me at the top of that mountain with a gun! And a return ticket! The second time I ran away I married the Duke and moved into his castle and pulled up the drawbridge behind me." She paused, remembering something which made her smile. "When I ran away from the Duke I hid myself in a lorry load of turnips destined for Madagascar!" But the smile soon faded. Sorrow crept onto her face. "Of course, look at me now – all that running only brought me to here, didn't it?"

"Do you want to run away again?" Alex asked. "What if we escaped together?"

"No, thank you! I'm tired of running. And you – well, now that your things are safe, you'd better get back to bed before they find out you're missing and send another howling search party after you."

Chapter Three

Alex spent the morning and much of the afternoon tidying up his aunt's and uncle's mess in their little office – a floating shack down on the log booms behind the Mill. It wasn't easy. They expected him to be a janitor and an expert filing clerk as well. The boards beneath his feet moved up and down in the waves from Aunt's little dozer boat, roaring around outside. Eventually his uncle came in and looked over the job he'd done, glowering like someone who hoped to find fault. "Knock off for now," he grunted. "There's somethin' your aunt said you gotta do – remember? You better get goin' and do it."

Apologize to everyone! Alex had not had very much practice at apologizing. The few times he'd hurt someone's feelings or broken a water glass by mistake, he had said "Sorry" without even thinking about it. He wasn't in any hurry now to get started at this.

If he had to apologize to the whole of Squabble Bay, he couldn't imagine starting without some advice from Frantic Freda. She was – at least she usually was – a friendly face.

She was not out at the end of the dock making her seashell jewelry, so Alex strolled down the beach in the grey drizzle to see if she was out collecting shells. But he didn't come across her anywhere. No rush. He kicked at stones and picked up starfish and leapt from log to log. He sat for quite a while on a piece of driftwood, pouring a scoop of gravel from one hand to the other, then he wandered in to town in case she was in one of the shops. No sign of Frantic Freda in the weight-lifting section of sporting goods. She wasn't in the rock section of the records store. She wasn't in the art section of the library either, where Alex thumbed through several books of fantasy art.

Eventually, he decided to go out to her rusty old sunken warship at the end of the breakwater, in case she was in her own home.

You had to watch your step along the breakwater if you didn't want to trip on the boulders and fall on your nose or stumble and slide into the sea. Still, the farther out into the bay he got, the more he wanted to look back at the land. Steep, tree-covered mountains disappeared up into cloud. The town was made up of row after row of houses climbing up the slope from the bay, blank picture windows staring out. Smoke stacks at the pulp mill poured dark clouds into the sky. There was the ugly sprawling school, with its muddy playing field. The downtown shops. Aunt and Uncle's little square store attached to the long trailer at the top of the steps to the beach. The Duchess-in-exile's sagging boat shed, protecting its hidden treasures.

Frantic Freda! In the shadows beneath the wharf, she was waving her arms at someone bigger than she was. It looked as if it might be the big stranger again.

Alex ran. He almost flew. *Thump, thump, thump,* down off the breakwater and onto the beach. Long-legged Alex ran down the length of one great log, then leapt the gap to another. On the narrower logs he had to hold out his arms for balance. Then he came crashing down the gravel slope to duck under the end of the wharf.

Freda whirled to face him, her fists up like a boxer. The stranger gawked. It *was* the big man! Wrinkles snaked across the front of his scalp. The red ostrich tail of hair drooped limply off the back of his head.

"Wait! Please!" The words shot out as Alex skidded to a stop in the gravel.

"What do you want?" said Freda. Every hair stood straight out in indignation.

"The Duchess-in-exile said – she told me you aren't a criminal." He was gasping for breath. "Do you have starving children?"

The big man's jaw dropped with surprise. Then he smiled. "Not a criminal! Well, that's decent of her."

Frantic Freda turned back to the stranger. "See!" she hissed. "What did I tell you?" She lifted one skinny leg and stomped her gumboot impatiently on the gravel.

The big man continued to grin. "Tell her I don't think she's much of a criminal either."

Freda looked at Alex but waved her arm at the stranger. "Go! Go!" Then quickly, to Alex: "You stay."

The big man looked sad, as though there were things he would like to say. Had he come back to raid Aunt's fridge? But he turned and moved up the slope, disappearing into a thicket of bush.

Alex could not hold his tongue. "Why were you mean to him? Just like the others!"

"I'm trying to *protect* him." Freda rushed past Alex, her gumboots thumping in the gravel as she started out along the beach. She held her hands up high and tight in front of her, her elbows oaring the air like wings. Her yellow-striped coat slapped around her bony knees. "He knows that. He's no dummy. If I don't protect the silly goose, who will?"

Following Freda along the breakwater, kicking at the weeds which grew in the cracks between boulders, Alex called out, "Why don't they want him around?"

She didn't speak until they had crossed the narrow plank between the last breakwater boulder and the deck of her ship. "Don't ask me!" She clomped across the deck and went in through one of the doors. Then she came out again. "There was a time you could actually hear people laughing in this town, believe it or not – thanks to him. Now you'd think they'd passed a law against it."

"Was he a clown?"

Frantic Freda did not answer. She raced down a flight of metal steps into a room where she had four coin-operated clothes dryers sitting in a row. Beyond them was a heap of gleaming seaweed which had been dropped through a trap door. Alex followed.

"Make yourself useful." She handed him a farmer's hay fork and used a second fork to start scooping up the wet seaweed into the dryers. "When I first moved here, he was a young fellow with a big talent for entertaining. A bit of a cut-up. Hold your fork like this and you'll get more to a load. The story they told was that he'd been kicked in the head by a horse or fell out of a tree, he wasn't all there – you know, one brick short of a load. Of course, that was all a big fat crock of meadow muffins. All he ever was was *different*."

She slammed the doors on the four dryers, then rooted around in her raincoat until she found a quarter. She put the quarter into the first machine, got it started, then kicked at the side of the machine until the quarter dropped to the floor. She put it into the second machine – and so on until all four of them were going. The room was filled with the roar of electric motors and the thumping of wet seaweed inside the drums. Freda shouted something at him but he couldn't hear. She came closer. "Move it, boy! This din will rattle the eardrums right out of your head."

They climbed up see-through steps and followed a narrow corridor and went down a second flight of stairs into a room like a scientist's laboratory. Tubs of bubbling liquid. Pipes. Inverted bottles connected to other bottles by tubes that twisted and looped like musical instruments. "Here's where the miracle happens," she called back to him. "This is where it gets turned into the bales of fertilizer for people's gardens. And here's where I make those packages of seaweed flakes for people I can hardly imagine over there in the Orient to put in their soup. Some day I'll be the richest woman in the country, between my seashell jewelry and my seaweed products." Great plastic bags were labelled: *Freda's Fantastic Fertilizer.* Small cardboard cartons said: *Freda's Fabulous Flakes.* "And without one speck of help from that pack of mudsharks in town."

Alex knew that the town people felt they were helping her out more than she would admit. He'd heard his aunt and uncle talk. "We let that crazy old bat live out on that boat and pretend we don't notice all the electricity she uses that's meant for the breakwater beacon. We buy her fertilizer for our gardens even though there's cheaper in the stores. But if we stop her, she'd only come up with something worse."

She marched down the aisle reading gauges, sticking her nose into jars and her finger into pots, giving tubes a good shake, turning taps on and off. "He had a way of giving them all a good time," she said. "Practical jokes. Teasing. Putting on one-man circuses. You should've seen him dance on the top of the Anglican steeple! He was also good at making fun of himself. How good are you at *that?*"

At the end of the aisle she turned and sat down on an overturned bucket. Through the portal above her head Alex could see out onto the strait. Seagulls sat on a floating log, complaining. "One day a certain blockhead started accusing the poor fellow of things. Nobody knew why. He said he smashed some expensive machinery. Said he did it on purpose."

"But – people believed him?"

"Those land-locked crustaceans will believe anything if they hear it often enough. You can't imagine how fast they turned against him. Mean? They were meaner than a sea lion poked at with sticks. Made his life just miserable. Criticized him. Stopped laughing at his jokes. Turned their backs when they saw him coming. One day he saw people cross the street to avoid him so he just walked off down that road and never came back."

"But he came back and you chased him off."

Freda shook her electric mop of hair impatiently. "You'd think he'd taken everybody's laughter with him. The saddest part is those crack-skulls didn't even notice what was missing. People just went sour. The Mill laid off half its workers and the biggest beer parlour in town burned down and Snarly Wilson got elected mayor. *Everything* went wrong! Most days now that SMILE on your cap is the only smile in town."

She put her hands on her knees and hoisted herself to her feet. "They haven't even figured out yet why they've gone sour." Elbows oaring, she stomped down the aisle between pots, and up the stairs.

"Aunt and Uncle want me to apologize to the whole of Squabble Bay."

"For what?" she shouted back without slowing down.

"The picture."

This time she stopped and turned to him. "Were you being honest when you drew it?"

"I drew how I felt."

"Did you want to hurt people?"

"I didn't mean anyone to see."

She swung around and started hurrying away again. "Well – it'd be a tideless Tuesday before they'd get an apology out of *this* old scrawny shorebird, let me tell you!"

"What if I didn't do it?"

"But then, I forget I'm not a kid – nobody cares if I get along with people or not. Depends if you want to go on putting your feet under their table, I guess. Say you're sorry for what you're sorry for – hurting feelings – and take your lumps for the rest." She stopped, panting from the rush. "Now, look – I'm going into the galley to rustle up some food. Will you stall around here forever, feeding off my superior common sense, or go out and get it over with?"

If he could not avoid this, Alex decided to begin with Mr. Hamilton, who never yelled. He was in his front yard – Alex could see him from out on the breakwater.

But when Alex had walked all the way in to the Hamilton house and started to say he was sorry, Mr. Hamilton said he didn't know what Alex was talking about, he was trying to solve this problem he had of his own. This small red-faced man with thick glasses was a reforestation expert for the logging company, in charge of planting millions of tiny trees up and down the sides of the logged-off mountains, yet he couldn't even keep the row of shrubs along his front lawn alive. "I'm the joke of Squabble Bay, I know it," he said. The whole row of knee-high cedars was the colour of rust. "And this is the fourth hedge I've planted here!"

"I bet my dad would know what to do if he was here," Alex said.

But Mr. Hamilton didn't seem to hear. "I studied trees for five years at university. I've planted over a hundred million seedlings up in the hills! I think they've trained a gigantic pack of dogs to pee on them just to make me look like a fool."

Behind the counter of Aunt's store Mrs. Pike wasn't a very good person to practise on either since she only shrugged her shoulders and pulled her face in towards the centre as if she'd just bit into a sour lemon. "I don't mind so much that you gave me four eyes in your picture" – she touched the glasses that sat on her nose – "but did you have to give me seven chins? I've only got three!" She turned to one side, to let him count. All three chins were jiggling from her silent laughter.

Just then Aunt stepped in through the door from behind Mrs. Pike, still wearing her safety hat. At this time of day she came up from the log booms to take over running the store. She pushed a button to open the cash drawer on the till and scowled while she counted the money.

"Well?" she said without looking up. "Finished already?" It was clear she was speaking to Alex. It was clear what she meant.

Mrs. Pike pressed her lips together and moved away to put on her jacket.

"Not yet," Alex said. "I'm sorry – "

The door opened, making the little bell tinkle. Aunt looked up and smiled an ugly smile. "Then here's a chance for you to practise your manners. Hello, Felicity."

Felicity Bogg and Billie Tonelli had come into the store, munching on chocolate bars. Bits of chocolate stuck to the crooked front teeth that slanted out of Felicity's mouth like the cow-catcher on an old train locomotive.

Billie Tonelli narrowed his eyes as if to study Alex under a microscope. "The great Rembrandt," he sneered. "Any more nasty pictures?"

Felicity bought a can of pop and pulled the tab open. She tipped up her face, dropped her jaw open and tilted the can so the orange drink poured into her mouth. "Let's have a look at those train tracks you got in your mouth."

Some people acted as if wearing braces was like owning a five-legged calf.

Alex opened his mouth and showed them off. He'd done it often enough before. "They're great for picking up radio stations," he said. "But dangerous in a lightning storm."

Felicity ambled across the room with a thumb hooked in her pants pocket as if she had three days with nothing to do but to get here. "I just want to see if you've got diamonds in there, your smile is so dazzling." She leaned close and scowled. *"Yeeee-uck!* Don't ever kiss a girl with those things, you're liable to rip off her face."

"If you're not buying anything, you better go on outside," Aunt said, slamming the cash register drawer. "Alex has something he wants to say to you."

"Old bag," Billie said under his breath as he moved towards the door.

But Felicity gave Aunt a wide grownup's smile and

50

sang out "Have a nice day!" so sweetly that even Aunt must have wondered if she meant it.

"You go too," Aunt said to Alex. "Out!"

Several people from Alex's class were lounging around the Burger Bungalow across the street. Jeff Padolski yelled, "Hey, McGuire, we're tryin' to figure out somethin' to do tomorrow. This holiday's a drag. Got any ideas?"

Alex looked at Jeff, who seemed friendly enough. He was just about the only one in the group who ever spoke to him. "I gotta work," Alex said. He knew there was a scared-rabbit look in his eyes. "They make me help them down at the Mill."

"What a crock!" said Billie Tonelli. "Them goons can't push you around. You don't want nothin' to do with us is all."

Jeff put a mud-soaked shoe on the bumper of someone's car and spat on the pavement. "We were thinking of taking Billie's old man's boat up the inlet to poke around in that abandoned float camp. Wanna come? Jake found a skull there once – didn't you, Jake? Somebody murdered."

Alex looked at Jeff. Did he mean it? Of course a thousand terrible things could happen, but maybe he would take a chance.

"Maybe he'd rather stay home and draw pictures," Jake Marinus said. He was the one who would grab the zipper of your fly and yank it down when he passed you in the hall. He had about eight black hairs growing on his upper lip and sometimes his voice would crack.

Jeff Padolski laughed. "Well, you gotta admit, he got old MacAdam just right. Gave her a turkey head!"

The others laughed. Even Jake Marinus. But Billie Tonelli narrowed his eyes at Alex. "He's probably too scared to come in the boat with us. What if it sprang a leak?"

Jake made his voice go high and whiny. "What if a great big whale leapt up and ate us? You think we can't hear you asking the teacher your questions? What if there's ghosts? Oh, I'm so scared!"

Alex looked at Jeff Padolski, who shrugged and turned up his palms.

Confused and disappointed, he pushed past Billie and started down the sidewalk. Felicity Bogg stepped back and looked hard at him as he passed her, but didn't say anything.

"Hey, McGuire!" This was Jake Marinus. You could hear the sneer in his voice. "Don't pee your bed, dreaming you're in our boat!"

The rest of them laughed. Alex's neck went hot but he tried to keep going as if he hadn't heard.

What if things never got any better for him here? What if he just kept on making more enemies?

Where was he going now? Not back to the breakwater ship. He could see it out there with the water lapping at its rusty hull. Frantic Freda would be busy cooking up another batch of her seaweed fertilizer without a single worry in her head. It must be nice to be so sure of things. People who made predictions just by sniffing the air and sticking a finger into the ocean had no reason to worry about anything. They *knew* – or thought they did. But Alex couldn't be sure of anything. What if his father never came back? What if he was stuck here forever? What if the whole town decided to punish him, and laughed at him wherever he went, and refused to forget that picture? What if they started a "Punish Alex Society" and held meetings to find new ways of making him miserable, and gave prizes to whoever came up with the worst punishment?

He thought of the Duchess-in-exile hiding in a truckload of turnips, heading for Madagascar. He had to get out of here.

Chapter Four

Aunt and Uncle were still arguing their way through breakfast when Alex climbed out the window of his bedroom. Once he was out on the street he ran as fast as he could, faster than he had ever believed he could run. His heart raced. Down past the store, up past the service station, out onto the highway.

The drafting board was strapped to the metal frame of Alex's blue nylon backpack. Inside he'd stuffed his paper and india ink and technical pens and completed pages of The Blade, along with a change of undershorts, a pair of socks, and a bag of cookies. His comics would be safe in the boat shed until Dad finally came home and sent for them. His tuque was in his pocket and his heavy jacket hung from the back of his belt – it would be real winter once he got away from the soggy coast.

At the first sound of a car he ducked behind a cedar tree and peered through the branches. Were they after him already? But it was only Mr. Hamilton in the yellow Company pickup. Alex stepped from behind the tree and stuck out his thumb.

Mr. Hamilton reached over and pushed open the passenger door. "You running a marathon or what?"

Alex climbed in, slammed the door and turned to look back through the window. No sign of Uncle Grump. No

sign of being followed. He closed his eyes. He couldn't very well tell him he intended to hitch-hike across the country. He couldn't tell him he intended to sleep in barns, and wash dishes in restaurants to pay for his meals.

"A drafting board," Mr. Hamilton said. "You must've got yourself a job as a survey engineer or you're heading out on a sketching expedition into the bush, like those famous painters."

"I'm heading out," Alex said.

They followed the winding paved road up the shoreline of the inlet, towards the mountains. "I could've stayed home today," Mr. Hamilton said, "but I can't keep away." He was such a short man that he was actually looking through the steering wheel. "Every morning I wake up thinking: What if every tree I've planted out there has died like the hedge in front of my house? Thousands of acres of little rust-coloured skeletons."

Over a bridge. Couldn't he drive any faster? Past a small farm. Up a long hill behind a slowpoke in an ancient Ford blowing clouds of blue oil smoke in their faces.

Alex thought it a bit silly for a man to be so worried about a bunch of little trees. "Why don't you just stick them in the ground and forget them?"

"Well, it takes time," Mr. Hamilton explained. You didn't just slap the seedlings into holes in the ground and expect them to grow into timber, he said. You gave them time to get over the shock. You dropped fertilizer from planes. You kept an eye on them, like any other crop. It took time for them to feel at home. Like people. "Oh, I know it's crazy for me to worry so much about them. But when I look at that hedge – and think I'm the man responsible for keeping the industry alive for the future – I break out in a cold sweat. This is as far as I can take you."

Seven logging truck trailers were parked along the side of the road – each a double set of wheels and a long tongue that rested in the rocks and mud and clumps of grass. The Company office was a squat yellow cement-block building. Pickup trucks were parked across the front of it, with CB radio antennas standing straight up from the roof of the cab. Should he look for one with the keys left inside – like kids in the movies – and try to drive it himself? How far would he get?

With his long strides Alex set out along the pavement and felt the old spring return to his step. Old-step-and-a-half! His good-mood walk. His dad had laughed about it. "You must have elastic feet, you actually go *up* and *u p!* Most people walk as if they're just dragging themselves through life."

A motorboat approached at such a speed that its prow slapped noisily on the waves, white spray arcing up behind it. Logs along the shoreline shifted and rocked from the wash. Someone behind the steering wheel waved. *"Hey-eeeeeeeeeeey!"* Abruptly, the boat tilted, cut a sharp curve and headed back this way. Whoever was driving slowed the motor, cruised closer, then cut it altogether and drifted shoreward.

Billie Tonelli. This must be his father's boat. He leaned on the steering wheel and flicked a cigarette butt out onto the sea. The salt chuck, they called it. It smelled fishy, like parts of the Byward Market.

"Wherever you're goin' we can get you there faster'n legs. Hop in!"

This was Jake Marinus. He was sitting back in the stern, drinking from a green can.

"Come on, McGuire! Get in!" Billie said. "We're scraping bottom. I'll get my arse kicked if we get scratches on the boat."

Billie Tonelli. Jake Marinus. He'd have felt better about it if Jeff Padolski were there. This road followed the inlet for just four or five more kilometres, then turned away. What harm would there be in catching a ride in a boat for that distance? Show these guys he wasn't the stuck-up nervous Nellie they thought he was. And give them something to think about when they found out later he'd run away. They would admire him then. They'd brag all over the school that they'd been the ones to help him escape.

But what if they'd been sent by Uncle to find him?

Don't be dumb. You couldn't imagine Billie Tonelli conspiring with any adult.

"How fast you going to go?"

"Slow as you want, McGuire, slow as you want. It's you that looks like somebody in a big hurry, not us."

He saw there were life jackets in the boat, though neither Billie nor Jake was wearing one. He could slip one on or hold onto one in case the boat tipped over.

He handed his backpack to Billie, tossed in his shoes and socks, then stepped into the water. It was cold at his ankles, and the barnacles on the rocks cut into his soles. He held out one hand to the rocking side of the boat and climbed inside.

"Hold on," Jake Marinus said.

The boat leapt up. If he hadn't been holding on, he could have fallen overboard.

But he wouldn't tell them he felt queasy in the stomach.

At this speed there wasn't just the noise of the motor and the slapping of the prow, there was also the wind.

"Might as well come and see the old camp with us, okay?"

"No!"

"Won't take long."

"Please! Just pull in, let me out here."

"Too late!"

The boat tilted beneath him and swung out from shore, pointing towards the opposite side. Mountains. Trees grew right down the steep slope to the water's edge. The world jerked up, slipped down, jerked up. The waves slapped beneath them. He was being taken out where he'd never been before. There was nothing over there but trees. Animals. He was being kidnapped by Billie Tonelli and Jake Marinus!

"But – " Alex said. "I was going home. I didn't say I wanted to see the shacks."

"Aw, relax." Jake shoved against Alex's shoulder.

Billie called back, "Have a little fun for a change, okay?"

"You wanted to come," Jake said, "but you were scared."

"You'll love it!" Billie called. "You can tell your city friends about it."

It wasn't only to the opposite shore they took him, it was much farther up the inlet. Here *both* sides were nothing but trees, cliffs, mountains. On the far side they spotted old buildings, a half-sunken wharf, a big A-frame made of logs leaning out over the water.

It was a float camp. The ground here was far too steep for buildings. The small cedar-shaked houses were out on log rafts, each linked to the shore by a narrow run of planks, connected to a neighbouring house by a single board. One building was submerged up to the windows. Roofs sagged. Glass was broken. Holes gaped in the walls.

"My old man grew up here," Jake Marinus said. "Look how much yard they had to play in!" A little space of planks around the sides of the house. How many kids were drowned?

"Look at this one," Jake said. "This was where they shot that man-eating cougar."

Alex watched the shoreline. Were there cougars? Bear? Wolves? All lived in these mountains, he knew that. But did they come down to shore? Would the sound of this motor attract them or scare them away?

"Cookhouse," Billie said, nosing the boat in against the raft, swinging to come alongside. "This is where the murder happened."

"Get out and give us a hand," Jake said.

Alex stepped out onto the slimy black planks of the raft. There was just enough room between the edge and the wall of the building for him to stand. Jake handed him a rope and showed him how to wrap it around a large rusty spike and knot it. Then both of the others got out.

"Padolski found a skull under those trees. Cook chopped a logger to death. C'mon, we'll go see where it happened."

You had to be curious about a thing like that, but how could you be sure these old planks weren't rotten? What if he or all of them fell through to the water?

They followed the wall to the corner, turned, and walked the narrow space between wall and water until they came to a doorway. The building sagged, pinched at one side as if a huge weight had pressed down from above. At the far end there was nothing but a big table, a couple of empty gas drums, and a scattering of shakes off the roof. And a marble.

Alex stepped in and picked it up. A steely. Maybe it

was only a mechanic's ball bearing, but he'd rather believe it had once belonged to some kid who played marbles on the floor of this shed. Where else could you play? The land was so steep you could never find a level spot large enough for a game of marbles.

"C'mon inside," Jake said, going ahead of them.

"The table," Billie said. He gave Alex's shoulder a push and went in.

"Look."

Both Jake and Billie seemed fascinated with the top of the table. Alex did not especially want to look but he would appear pretty silly if he refused.

The wooden table top was a mess of gashes from what might have been an axe. Some were so close together they made strange patterns, but all were deep enough to make the muscles in your stomach tighten.

"We figure Cook chopped him to pieces here and threw him in the chuck," Billie said.

"With his meat cleaver," Jake added.

Both of them looked at Alex with their eyes made big while they said this. What were they hoping he would do? Cry? Run away?

"But – how do you know these aren't just from chopping up meat?"

"Stupid," Billie said. "Look at the blood!"

Dark puddles had soaked into the wood. It was enough to make something cold start at the base of your spine and work its way up.

What if the cook had hidden out here all these years with his cleaver? What if he was looking at Alex this minute through one of those cracks between the boards? What if he sprang out now, giving a blood-thirsty yell, and came after him?

"Did they catch him?" Alex asked.

"Of course not," Jake said. "Nobody knows where he is."

"Did he just do it once?"

"Who knows?" Billie said. "Plenty of people have gone missing. Maybe he drags them off before he hacks them up."

Suddenly they both took off – ran out through the door and around the corner, yelling and hollering as though they thought the cook was after them with his cleaver. Along the outside of the building went their shouting, and around another corner.

Then their voices were drowned out by the sound of the boat's motor starting up. Realizing what this meant, Alex ran after them.

Too late. They'd already untied the rope, and the boat had moved away from the raft. They'd tossed his backpack onto the boards. And his shoes. What did this mean? One sock floated on the stirred-up water.

"So long, McGuire. Don't be scared of the ghosts!"

Blue smoke from the motor. They were gone. Just like that. Swung out into the open water, laughing, waving at him and speeding up.

They would come back. They'd have to come back. They were just trying to give him a scare. They would leave him long enough to throw a good scare into him and then they would come back and rescue him. He was a million miles from anywhere.

But would they have thrown him his shoes if they'd planned to come back? They'd headed straight out to the middle of the inlet and turned to head in the direction from which they had come. The *slap, slap, slap* of the prow and the roar of the motor faded and eventually died out altogether.

He was stuck here. Abandoned. If this were the

opposite side of the inlet, he could walk along the coastline until he came to civilization, even if it took weeks. He could walk, swim where the shoreline was too steep, he could paddle on logs. Get out at last, nearly starved. Tell his story to the papers and be a hero.

But who knew how much farther the inlet went before you came to the end and could go around to start back down the opposite side? This was going to be one of those stories you read about in the papers. A hungry bear would stalk him. Watch him. He would get thinner by the day. He'd try to live off the land but the only berries he'd find would turn out to be poisonous. Eventually a cougar would drop down out of a tree onto his neck and finish him off, a light snack. No one would know for years.

By then Billie Tonelli and Jake Marinus would be adults, living far away; no one would know where.

How would Night Crawler handle this? How would The Blade?

He put his shoes on and threw away his one remaining sock. Then he hoisted his backpack up between his shoulder blades. Sooner or later he was going to have to move or see if there was something inside one of these houses he could make use of. A boat maybe. A little dinghy, an old rowboat that he could get into the water.

He wouldn't think about that cook. He wouldn't let himself wonder if the cook was still around. That was stupid. That was exactly what those two wanted.

He walked the sagging bridge of planks to the beach, then followed a walkway of planks along the high-tide line until he came to another bridge and followed it too, out to a raft with two buildings on it. Both empty. Both shells. You could look up and see plenty of sky through the holes. In this climate you couldn't even count on a place like that to keep you dry.

There must be a dozen buildings here, all on rafts, most of them collapsing, empty except for useless bits of lumber or rusted metal cans. One raft with its tilted shed had been washed right up on the shore. Above the high-tide line it angled awkwardly, one corner jammed in the fork of a two-trunked tree. Must've been broken free and blown in a storm.

Birds. Gulls. Some wheeled in the air, some padded in the water along the beach. Crying, as if for help. What did they know about needing help? They could take off and fly whenever they wanted; nobody could leave them marooned where they couldn't get out. Unless they clipped their wings.

Around the corner there were still more rafts, more buildings. He didn't go into them all. But one, far up the row, seemed in better shape than the others. The walls were upright, solid looking. The door was closed. One of its windows even had glass. Out at the end of its damp plain walkway it looked like a house that refused to fall down or sag or give in to the weather and time, as these others had done.

Whoever had lived in this one had left everything behind. A stove. A table. Chairs. A narrow bed with blankets still on it.

Nothing had rotted, nothing had rusted.

Even a mayonnaise jar with paint brushes in it, and some kind of cloudy liquid.

And a plastic bathtub that had no taps, no drain hole. Painted a shiny red. You could smell the paint. Fresh.

He was on the verge of touching the paint to see if it was wet when he realized what all this meant.

Someone was living here.

And behind him, right now, someone was breathing.

He turned. A figure stood in the doorway. A figure that ducked out of sight. The mad cook? Or was it only his imagination? Nobody needed to tell him how much mischief a person's imagination could do. But to conjure up a man, and *hear him breathe?* Alex's heart thumped so loudly it seemed to be rattling the inside of his head. There was no other way out of this place unless he went through one of those windows and dropped into the water.

Chapter Five

Again the man appeared in the open doorway. Tiny eyes blinked in a large face; a small mouth twitched this way and that. Almost smiling, almost pouting, almost forming an angry line. It was the man they'd chased from the store! The man they'd treated like a criminal. Maybe he *was* a criminal!

Was it safe to breathe? Before Alex could decide, the man had disappeared again. Feet went thumping down the floating planks. Water sloshed and splashed.

When Alex went to the door, he saw only the quick movement of a leg, a foot, disappearing into the next shack, a tilted wreck with broken windows. Was he getting a gun? A meat cleaver? What if he was about to release a pack of wild dogs?

But no dogs came leaping and snarling out the door. No gun barrel slid out through the window. A gust of wind blew through the trees on the shore, disturbing the higher boughs. Alex went back inside the shack and looked out the window. The large man was in the tilted window of the other shack now, looking this way. Planning an attack? His mouth was moving; he seemed to be saying something.

Alex pushed the window open.

"State your business," the man shouted. Eight or ten

metres of slapping water separated them. "What are you doing here?" He sounded dangerous.

"I was only – " Alex's voice was barely a whisper.

"Trespasser!" the man shouted.

No dogs. No guns. No hand grenades yet.

"Don't you recognize me? I've been kidnapped!"

"Who'd kidnap you? Who'd pay a fortune to get *you* back?"

Nobody ever would. His father might, if he knew. If he found a fortune somewhere in that South American jungle. If he could get here in time.

"And where are the kidnappers now? Are they terrorists or what?"

"They just left me here," Alex said. "I'm marooned."

"D'you suppose it's all right if I come back inside my own home or do I have to write ahead for a reservation? Is the place surrounded with cops waiting to throw me in chains?"

"No, sir. If there were, they'd be after me!"

At this the man stuck his head through the broken window. "You're a criminal?" You could hear the word "criminal" echoing off up the inlet and into the mountains.

"You'd think I was," Alex said, "the way some people act."

"Well, hold your fire, I'm coming over." The man's head disappeared from the window. In a moment footsteps came thumping along the floating planks. Water sloshed and slapped. Alex's heart began racing again. He turned to face the door and moved back against the farthest wall.

The thumping slowed down outside. The big man entered carefully, his eyes checking out every corner of this room. He put one foot inside the door, then the other; but he kept a hand on either side of the frame. Then he looked at Alex a good long while with a steady frown. Alex said nothing. What could he say? The man looked fierce, strong enough and mad enough to pull this building down on them if he wanted. His hands were the size of baseball mitts. He glared at Alex as though he could see right into his skull and didn't much like what he saw.

"I'm the one – " Alex began, but his voice would not quite work. The man frowned harder. Suspicious, impatient. Alex cleared his throat. "I'm the one who . . . said you could have my aunt's fridge. I mean, the milk and stuff in it. Maybe you forgot."

The frown loosened a little, shifted, became softer. The mouth remained tightly closed but spread out slowly into a grin, an embarrassed sort of grin. "You and I just can't help bumping into each other, it seems."

Alex said, "I'm sorry about my aunt."

The man shrugged. "I'm sorry about your aunt myself." He grabbed a metal pot from the table and scooped up water from a pail on the floor. He drank from the pot, eyeing Alex suspiciously, then poured the rest of the water into a kettle on the stove.

"Did you find any food?"

"Luckily there's the odd fish that swims right under my house, begging to be thrown into the frying pan. Once in a while a boy or girl stumbles in. You'd be surprised how many meals you can get out of a twelve-year-old. Salt some. Smoke some. Dry some. Eat the liver while it's fresh. Use the fingers for bait to catch more fish. Throw the bones to the wolves."

Of course he was kidding, but his smile was a private one – not a smile he would share with Alex. He didn't look at Alex and wink. Down on his knees he concentrated on laying out a criss-cross pyramid of sticks and bits of bark in the firebox of the little stove.

Alex took a deep breath. It was important not to sound scared. "You keep your boat tied up beneath the house?"

"No boat."

If he had no boat, how could he have got into town?

"If I had a boat I would've sunk her myself. So I wouldn't be tempted to leave." He blew on a tiny thread of smoke that smouldered in the twigs and shavings and bits of bark and dried leaves.

"But – " Alex's mouth was dry. His tongue had forgotten how to do its job. "Why are you here, sir?" You had to be careful to make sure some adults didn't think you were being pushy.

The smouldering burst into tiny flames that licked at the twigs.

"When I first came out here, it was just to feel sorry for myself. Then I discovered I liked it."

"But – "

The fire had caught. The big man slammed the door on the front of the stove, slid a handle that opened a small square hole and stood up. "I went out – remember? Can you imagine I'd ever want to go out again?"

"I'm not going back to that town either, I'm running away."

"You kidding?" The man narrowed his eyes to glare at Alex. "I'm not helping a kid run away from his home."

"It's a prison. If you take me back, I'll just run away again."

The big man's forehead wrinkled up. "Which of those shacks you want to camp in then? I've got the only one that doesn't leak."

Alex moved to the window. Outside, water stretched away down the inlet. There was the tilted shack the man had run to. "How bad is that one?"

"Not too bad if you've got one leg longer than the other – there's a slant to the floor. Tie your camp stove and bed and extra clothes to the wall at the higher end. And yourself too at night, to keep from rolling down into the indoor pool. Where'd you put your camping gear?"

"I've just got this." Alex motioned to his backpack. "I was running away to the city, not the bush."

"Well, the bush is where you are. You'd better go pick yourself a house. I'm heating myself some soup and you can have a taste once you're settled. Made from dogfish heads and toadstools and elk's milk and ears from the Vancouver Island marmot."

Stooping down with his head inside a wooden chest, he turned to look at Alex and winked.

Alex visited the other floating shacks. The tilted one next door was partly under water, as the big man had said. The next one had no roof at all. Farther along the floating planks he came to a shack with a roof, but most of the boards had been pulled off its walls, probably for firewood. Bare studs stood around it like prison bars. Another shack still had its walls and even its windows, but the roof had collapsed as though a space ship had landed on top.

Finally Alex returned to the big man's shack, which now smelled of both soup and paint. The man was down on his knees brushing paint onto the outside of his bathtub. Stop-sign red. "This is my fifth coat."

A red bathtub without plumbing! Alex looked out the window. The water was choppy. Even some whitecaps farther out. Wind.

"You don't know how much trouble it is," the man said, "trying to make sure no one finds me. Every time I light a fire I'm taking a chance." He frowned and stopped painting to look at Alex. "They'll come back, those people who dumped you here. Someone'll miss you. That aunt. A grownup like me – well, nobody misses. But a boy."

Uncle Grump. Aunt Gruff. He saw them turning the town upside down looking for him. Uncle would be yelling threats. Forty years labour on the log booms! One hundred lashes with a bull whip! Ninety-eight years on some tiny island where there was nothing but thousands of messy nesting birds! Make the boy wear dresses to school, chain him to his desk and force him to speak nothing but Chinese!

"If they find me I won't tell them you're here," Alex said.

The eyes narrowed. The big man pulled a hand out of the pocket of his overalls and tossed something to Alex. A piece of bubble gum in a soiled and tattered wrapper. "I can blow a bubble twice as big as my head. How about you?"

"You kidding?" Alex said, looking down at the little package in his hand. He opened his mouth to show his braces. "It'll be another year before I'm allowed to chew gum."

"Oh." The big man grinned and snatched the bubble gum back. "You've got those cages in your mouth. To keep all the little white birds from flying out." He put the paint brush in the jar of liquid and stood up, grunting. "But I promised you some of my soup." He went to the stove and poured the thick liquid into two cracked bowls on the table. "Grab that spoon and dig in. And tell me – which of those palaces out there have you picked for yourself?"

Alex pulled up a wooden box to the table and looked into the bowl of soup. Dark things floated. But he was hungry. If the man ate some, he would try to eat some himself. "I can't stay in any of those shacks," he said. "I guess you'd better take me across to the road."

The big man sat at the table and slurped up the soup. He seemed to think it was wonderful. "Find yourself a corner in here for tonight, so long as you don't touch things that aren't yours. Tomorrow you can pick a shack and start ripping boards off the others to patch it up. In a few weeks it'll feel like home. Now eat up."

"Did you ever work here when it was a logging camp?" Alex said. "As a cook maybe?"

"Taste my soup. Do you think they'd hire someone who couldn't do better than that?"

Alex lifted a spoonful to his lips. "Dogfish heads?" He stuck his tongue out for a taste. "Toadstools?" Toadstools were supposed to be poisonous. "Marmot ears?"

"Campbell's Mushroom," the big man said. "With just a little of this and that added for local flavour." He finished up his bowl with a great sigh and went to the stove. He poured water from the steaming kettle into a teapot and put an empty cup on the table.

While the big man sipped his tea, Alex looked around this room. Square. Not much furniture. Light came in through cracks between the wall boards, grey unpainted wood which had aged and weathered and started to rot. "Why are you putting so many coats of paint on that bathtub when you haven't painted anything else in this room?"

The man looked surprised. "I never noticed. Walls are just walls, but a bathtub's different! I suppose once I get this finished I could decorate the old shack up a little. There's some blue, I think. And a can of yellow I found on a shelf in the cookhouse." He looked around the room and up at the ceiling. "That drawing board you've got strapped to your pack – you an architect or what? Or do you think you're some kind of artist?"

"The kind that gets in trouble," Alex said. "There's a whole town back there mad at me because they don't like what I drew."

The big man raised his eyebrows at that. "That's quite an accomplishment. I don't know of a single person that was ever burned at the stake for his pictures. Some starved, I guess. Most were ignored. Whatever you drew, it must've been pretty bad."

"Them."

"Them! And you're still alive to tell it? You must be pretty fast on your feet."

"I was just doodling. Cartoons. But it got shown around."

"And nobody laughed. Sounds familiar." He thought a moment, serious. Then his face brightened. "Well, look – all these blank walls are just waiting for someone like you to do something with them. Slap a few of your cartoons up there and see if I laugh or get mad."

Alex looked at the dull grey walls, so old they were stained with dark water marks, so rainsoaked their surface had gone soft and furry. "Usually I don't do cartoons," he said. "Mostly I like to do superheroes."

The big man raised an eyebrow. "Superheroes can't be funny?"

"Superheroes have to save lives."

"Well, it must be tough on those fellows, taking themselves so seriously all the time. My own hero when I was a boy was Uncle George. He never rescued anyone in his life, but he was funny. Every time he came in the house my poor old mother would end up rolling on the floor, laughing. All of us would, at his antics. He'd show up just whenever things were bad, and he'd never come in through the door like anybody else. He always came in through a window, usually with his clothes on inside out or upside down or backwards. Usually he would get himself stuck in the window and the whole family would have to spend half an hour trying to get him inside. Sweaters unravelled behind him, pants peeled off, shoes turned out to be made of elastic that stretched halfway through the house. He never got through a meal at our table without telling us stories about his loony neighbour that would make our stomachs hurt too much from laughing to care that there wasn't any dessert. Go ahead. Do anything you want so long as you make me smile. No steely-eyed big-jawed supermen for me. If we don't like what you do, we can always paint over it."

When the big man had gone back to painting his bathtub, Alex sat at the table, looking out the window. "That crazy cook who murdered somebody here," Alex said, "have you seen him around?"

The man laughed. "You believed that story?"

"But – I saw the table."

"You saw the table. Did it speak?"

"But – they told me they found a skull."

"People got killed in these camps all right, but not from lunatic cooks. Falling trees and broken machinery did the job."

"I thought you might be him, hiding out." Alex wasn't sure he should say this. "I thought I'd be chopped up in bits."

"Well, there you are – still in one piece. It shows what

imagination can do. Maybe you could put yours to better use. Do something about those walls."

Why not? It was something to do. Alex took a narrow paint brush out of the jar of turpentine and stood back to size up the section of wall between the front door and the corner. What did he see, what could he imagine? Nothing. Just the dull furry surface of old wood.

He thought of Uncle Grump down on the log booms. "You're walking like there's eggs under your feet," his uncle would say. "You scared of the whole blasted world? Try to act like a man!"

He used a screwdriver to open a can of blue paint and a piece of kindling to stir it. Then he dipped his brush in the paint and drew one line up the wall – up and curved over and down. He put a big ugly foot out each side at the bottom. A thick solid stump with feet. He put a safety hat on top, then sketched a beard and drew a straight line above the beard – a scowling brow. A thick, mean-looking stump.

The big man looked up at it and frowned. "Is that supposed to be funny?"

"It isn't?"

Alex looked at the drawing a moment, then painted giant boots over those feet, drew several sharp spikes under the soles, and put a whirling log beneath one foot. Then he painted a great big surprised hole for a mouth, and tiny flailing arms to show the log had gone out of control and his uncle was about to fall in.

He dipped the brush again and drew another stump with feet beside the first – a little shorter, a little wider – and put another safety hat on top, this one falling off. Then he sketched a pair of brows like a V, and a sweetly smiling mouth. It wasn't difficult to paint the hands which had obviously just given Grump

a shove and started the log spinning.

"*Ahhhhhh!*" The big man clapped. "Now that's funny. Maybe even those two would laugh if they saw it."

Alex was pretty sure they would not.

The big man shook his head, still smiling. "Now see what you can do with *me.*"

Alex looked at this man. How could he do something like that? "Not now," he said, putting the brush back into the jar.

"You could draw me in my bathtub," the man said. He looked prepared to step inside, though the paint was wet. "I could put the motor on and you could draw me racing it over the waves."

Racing it over the waves?

"You could draw me holding my winner's trophy after I've won a race," he said. "Champion of the entire world. If it's superheroes you want, then how about Mr. Super-bathtub-racer?"

"You mean this thing is really the boat you came here in? This *tub?*"

The man nodded, trying to hide a grin. "This *thing,* as you call it, was once famous all up and down the coast. So was this person you're looking at."

"If you were so famous, would I know your name?"

"The Top Banana. Nobody's come along to challenge that yet. Any objections?"

"No, sir," Alex said.

The Top Banana looked up at the ceiling crossbeams and the slanted rafters. "Right across the strait to the mainland. Hundreds of us! Four or five hours in the open water. The whole town used to go down-Island by the busload on the day of the race, to cheer me on at the starting line. The photographers! Pictures in every paper. I was their hero. The Champion. The Top Banana! Mrs. Pike would slip chocolate bars into my grocery bag because I made her laugh."

"But – why did you leave? If they liked you so much."

The Top Banana looked at Alex as if he were trying to see right inside him. Then it seemed as though he were really not looking at Alex at all but at something inside himself. And listening hard. "Wind," he said. "Storm coming up."

"How bad will it be?"

"It can get pretty bad this time of year. We don't call them hurricanes exactly, but they can be pretty darn close."

"Will we be safe?"

"So long as everything's nailed down. So long as the cables hold – tied around trees on the shore. You want me to tie you to a tree?"

"What if we're blown out to sea?"

The Top Banana didn't seem worried. "Haven't you always wanted to visit Japan?"

"I'd rather go by plane."

"So would I, frankly, but at least this would be a lot cheaper."

Chapter Six

When Alex awoke during the night the swinging motion of the raft beneath them had got a little rougher, the breaking of the waves against the shack a little noisier. Wind roared in the trees and rattled the door and windows. The promised storm had arrived. Either that or some monster was throwing a fit: howling, thumping, shaking up the world.

It was dark. Lying in the Top Banana's cot, Alex could not see across the room to where the big man was sleeping in his bathtub. Was he still there?

What if this were an emergency? What if someone should be checking the cables that kept them tied to the trees?

"Are you awake?" Alex spoke into the darkness.

A gust of wind slapped against the wall behind the cot and made strange whistling noises along the cracks. Cold air shot through the house.

From across the room came a snuffling sound and a series of grunts.

Alex called a little louder. "You awake?"

Something crashed outside. Perhaps a tree had fallen. Gull screams went flying off in the wind, spreading alarm.

The snoring interrupted itself with a loud snort, then

more snuffling. Then silence. Then the Top Banana's voice said, "I'm stuck to the tub."

"Stuck?"

"Some of the paint wasn't dry." There was a sound like an adhesive strip being torn from skin. "Only my shoulder, but don't worry, I've ripped it free. There's probably a little paint on my face, but it'll wear off eventually."

The whole house shuddered from a gust of wind.

"Now what are you doing awake? If you're not going to make use of the only decent bed in the place, you should give it to someone who will."

"It's the hurricane," Alex said. "Listen."

"Don't be scared of a little wind. Relax. Just ride 'er out."

If Dad knew about this storm, would he be worried? Probably not. He would think that Alex was safely asleep in his uncle's extra bed.

"You think my dad'll come back when his two years are up?"

It was the kind of question you could ask out loud only in the dark, in the middle of a storm, far from home, with a stranger. Nowhere else. Even then, you wished right away that you'd kept your big mouth shut.

For a moment it seemed as if the Top Banana hadn't heard. Good. What could he answer anyway? What could he possibly know?

But he did answer. Or speak, at least, if it wasn't what you could call an answer. "Fathers usually do," he said. "Eventually." A pause, and then he added, "Of course some of them never do. So what am I talking about? You know your old man, I don't, you should have a better idea about whether he'd just take off and never come back. Is that the kind of thing he does? Tell me about him."

"Maybe some other time," Alex said.

His throat would hurt if he tried to talk about his dad. It already hurt.

Alex lay on the Top Banana's cot and stared into the dark. Pretend you're on a ship. An ocean liner. A cruise ship, taking you somewhere wonderful. South America.

Rustle. Thump. The Top Banana was changing position inside the tub. "You asked me why I ran away? Your uncle fired me. I'd ruined a lot of equipment down on the booms. He told everyone I did it on purpose." His voice was dreamy in the dark. It was like staying overnight at Mark's place, except for the way this whole building was heaving about. Mark always waited until you were lying in the dark to tell something important. "They all said, 'Don't be silly, he couldn't have done a thing like that on purpose, not our Champion.' So your uncle got madder and told worse things. One day I went into the store and Mrs. Pike said no more free chocolate bars."

"The Duchess-in-exile told me about you when she found me in her shed," Alex said. "She thought I was an assassin sent by the Royal Family, but I didn't even have a gun."

A huge sigh from the tub. "That woman was like a mother to me, even when everyone else turned against me. She was always my best audience – shrieked with laughter."

"The Duchess-in-exile shrieked?"

"All the time. She would laugh until she cried, until she was helpless. Wasn't she nice to you?"

"She didn't mind too much when I snuck into her shed. I never had a mother," Alex said. "Did you?"

The Top Banana remained quiet for a long time. "I

don't remember." Outside, waves slammed at the raft. Trees creaked and groaned, rubbing against one another. "Things should look better in the morning. Let's get some sleep."

"I hope you don't stick to the paint for good," Alex said, but the big man was already snoring in the dark.

When Alex awoke again it was because he'd been thrown against the wall. It felt as though the storm intended to pick them right up and hurl them across the world. The door swung open, slammed closed, swung open again. Sea water sloshed across the floor, foaming, slapping bits of weed and wood against the wall. The world had gone crazy – bucking, howling, rattling, probably foaming as well.

Rain blew in the window when he sat up to see what was happening. His T-shirt and undershorts were sprayed. Though it was daylight now, the rain was coming down so hard you could barely see land. Water stood up in mountainous peaks which were slapped by the wind into riotous sheets of spray.

They were in the middle of the churned-up inlet, far from the blurred land, probably heading for the open sea. The logs of the raft beneath them made a terrible creaking sound.

"They're separating!" the Top Banana's voice called from somewhere.

Alex leapt to his feet. The floor of the house was dangerously tilted. "Where are you?"

"Up here!"

The Top Banana looked down from the roof. A whole section of shakes must have blown away. In his overalls he sat straddling a slanted rafter. Rain slashed against him. His clothes were drenched. His face streamed water. "Just trying to figure our prospects before I woke you!" he called down. "The raft beneath us is falling apart!"

What if they smashed into a rock?

What if they sank?

"Are we going to die?" Alex asked.

"Not without a fight. Hang on."

A sudden jolt threw Alex against the bed, sent him sprawling, sliding towards the door. Everything in the room was sliding with him – cot, table, chairs, even the stove, whose metal chimney had fallen in pieces to the floor. He did not shoot out through the open door, though, but slammed up against the wall, making his shoulder hurt.

Again the terrible creaking beneath them. The scream of rusty spikes being wrenched from the logs?

Up on the roof the Top Banana roared, "There goes another one. Hang on!"

This time Alex was flung back and hurled against the wall where his cot had been. His T-shirt was soaking wet now, his undershorts ripped. He checked to make sure his SMILE cap was still on his head.

"Don't move!" the Top Banana yelled. "The logs have gone out from under this half of the house!"

Slowly, with a great deal of creaking and popping, that end of the house sagged. Dark water came up through the cracks in the floor. Up the legs of the bed. Over the blankets, which lifted for a moment, almost floating, then sank.

The stove disappeared. Only up at the high end was there any floor left above water.

The Top Banana dropped off the roof and set his feet on a ceiling crossbeam, his hands still on the rafters.

"Don't move," he said. "Stay there."

Alex clung with both hands to the two-by-four stud.

The roof seemed to be sagging too, as if a huge weight were squeezing it down towards the floor. Then something snapped.

The ceiling crossbeam.

Beneath the Top Banana's feet it sagged, split open, fell apart, to leave the man dangling by his hands, his feet kicking at air.

Then, suddenly, the Top Banana dropped.

For one split second his small blue eyes looked into Alex's; his mouth open, his ostrich tail of hair straight up and waving like seagrass. Then he slipped under the water.

Alex let go of the two-by-four and plunged down the slope. Up to his knees. Up to his crotch. Where had the big man gone? What if he'd gone right out through the hole, gone under the house?

But someone was heaving beneath the surface. A body. Alex ducked, grabbed at something – a shoulder?

The Top Banana's head burst free from the water, spitting, gasping. His shoulders, streaming water. His arms.

"Climb!" he yelled. "Get back up to the high end!"

Alex used the studs of the outside wall like a sideways tilted ladder to help move back up the slope and out of the water. He grasped the Top Banana. Each held the other's wrist. Slowly Alex helped him pull himself free.

The wind howled in the naked rafters. Waves slammed against the building. The floor shuddered. Alex was cold, wet. Maybe the entire earth was throwing this fit, using wind to help it toss all people and buildings and trees and everything else right off its back. Tired of the whole blessed lot. Deciding to start all over again from scratch once everything alive had been flung out into space.

Beside him the Top Banana hauled great noisy breaths into his lungs.

Then he laughed. Laughed? Well, tried to. Coughed. Spat. Laughed again. "I guess you were right – a plane would've been a better way to travel! You see Japan out there yet?"

"No. I guess I don't want to either."

"What! Don't want to wash up in the Exotic East?"

"I'm out of place enough in Squabble Bay! How long would I last where I don't even know how to speak?"

"Grovelling and begging for mercy is just about the same in any language." Still breathing hard, he grinned broadly at Alex. "But take my advice – okay? If we get there, don't go deciding to draw their picture. I haven't got the strength for another escape."

Chapter Seven

By mid-morning the worst of the storm seemed to have passed, but they were still afloat in the middle of the inlet. The house was angled as if it intended to take a dive for the bottom, and seemed to hang heavily on the water's surface, or just below it. But the sea hadn't yet decided whether to swallow or spit it out.

The Top Banana, sitting with his back to the wall where the rain didn't reach, looked as if he hadn't the strength to wiggle a toe, but he seemed to think the whole thing was funny. "Just holler when you get your first look at a rice field." His red hair, which had drooped while it was wet, was beginning to stand up again like an ostrich tail. A small patch of bathtub paint was stuck to one ear.

"What if we *do* get blown a million miles from land?"

The Top Banana closed his eyes. "Listen, it can blow us anywhere it likes just so long as it doesn't blow us away from our own intelligence. Please hang onto yours!"

Alex moved carefully over to the window. The sky was dark, still spilling down rain. Trees along the shoreline had been torn out by their roots.

"But – what if we smash into something? What if this house slides off the raft and sinks? What if – if there's nothing left to hang onto?"

The Top Banana looked at his big, spread-out feet for a minute, then looked at Alex in a tilted sideways manner, as if he weren't sure he ought to say what he was about to say. "What if the sky should fall? What if the Queen woke up one morning with a long grey beard? Try to finish one of your *what if* sentences with a good idea for a change!"

What if they dived in and swam? But then, what if they drowned?

His feet, out at the ends of his legs, weren't half the size of the Top Banana's feet. Those big black shoes could serve as kayaks for a pair of adventurous rabbits – but not for them.

"What if we used a couple loose boards for paddles and tried to swing it towards the shore?"

The big man laughed heartily. "You must have a giant's muscles inside that shirt. I confess, I haven't."

"What if we set out in the bathtub?" It hadn't slid down to the submerged part of the room. No. That would be even more dangerous.

The big man looked pleased and slapped his big open palms where his knees showed through the holes in his overalls. "Not a bad idea." He started to hoist himself to his feet. "Let's see if all that bashing around has ruined the engine."

"I hear a boat coming," Alex said. He grabbed his pants down off the nail and pulled them on, cold and damp on his legs.

The Top Banana dropped to the floor. Alex crawled to the window. A speedboat was coming this way.

The Top Banana's great long face had grown longer. Did they really want to be rescued now? As far as

Alex was concerned, that depended on who was racing towards them.

Gradually, as the boat drew nearer, Alex spied someone standing up at the rear. It was Frantic Freda, her yellow raincoat and wild hair flapping out behind her. She wore a backwards captain's hat crammed down on the top of her head. Holding her long nose up to the wind, she searched the sea through her binoculars.

Soon he could see Felicity Bogg at the wheel. This was almost as bad as discovering that his aunt and uncle were in the boat.

The motor died. The boat nosed in to planks just outside the tilted door. The Top Banana hid behind the door on his hands and knees.

"I bet you wish you never drew that stupid picture!" Felicity called. "Look where it's got you now. Anybody told you yet you're floating?"

She tied the boat to a large rusty spike and leapt onto the raft. "In case you haven't noticed, this floor is angled like the Titanic's just before she vanished." She spoke without moving her lips much. Was there something wrong with her mouth?

Frantic Freda stepped inside, sniffing the air. She wore two, four, eight big pieces of her own seashell jewelry down the front of her yellow coat. An Admiral's decorations. "The things you run into when you haven't got a gun," she said. "A drowned rat that forgot to leave the ship." She held onto the wall and worked her way down the slope to stare into the water. The stove, the table, the chairs and a wooden chest were all crammed together and mostly submerged, faintly visible beneath the water. "Just because you've been found doesn't mean you ought to relax, boy. Things could get even worse." She tilted back her head to look up through the great gaps in the roof. A few drops of rain fell on her face.

"Look around you," Alex said. "How could it get any worse?"

Freda surveyed the chaos. Alex thought that she might be chuckling. Then she smiled. "Your uncle. Remember him? That charming son of a gun is probably hot on our trail by now. Eager as a bloodhound. Breathing fire. Ready to blowtorch your little pointed rear."

She was right. It could be worse.

"The town's in a mess," Felicity said, staying close to the doorway. She spoke with one hand to her mouth. "Your aunt and uncle's logs are all over the place – in people's bathroom windows, standing on end against fences, blocking the streets, resting like bridges from roof to roof, and slanting up from the playground to the top of the school. Everyone's mad at them."

Alex smiled to think of how mad everyone must be at his uncle and aunt. Then he sobered to think of how mad his uncle and aunt must be at him. They would blame him for everything if they could – even the storm!

"You think that's funny?" Freda said, opening and closing a broken window. "Last night in the middle of everything, Jake Marinus decided to tell what they did with you. Police are out. Search and Rescue helicopters in the air." She yanked at a loose board in the wall, then looked up towards the sky, sniffing. "Another big blow tonight – maybe sooner."

Felicity rolled her large round eyes. "It wasn't my idea, I'll tell you that for sure." She pointed at Freda. "She forced me!"

"Commandeered," said Freda like an Admiral of the Fleet. "Conscripted!" She thunked the heels of her yellow gumboots together and saluted. "In times of emergency, if a country's attacked, the government can take over private boats in a minute and put them into action."

"The country's been attacked?" Alex said.

"Dummy!" Felicity said. "And she's not the government either, whatever she thinks. But that didn't stop her from just *taking over*. You ever tried to argue with her?"

Alex watched Freda open one cupboard door after another. What was she looking for?

"I had a premonition," Freda said. "I crawled out from under the table when the storm was over and I *knew*: that long-legged Back-East shell-pickin' beach-orphan kid is in trouble. I smelled it in the air. Or maybe in the water slopping around my feet. That storm left tonnes of seaweed all over my boat, by the way. It'll make me my fortune!"

At that moment the Top Banana crawled out from behind the door. "Knights in armour look a bit different these days than they used to," he said. He grunted as he got to his feet, a sheepish smile on his face.

Felicity jumped at the sound of his voice. "Who else is hiding in here?"

Freda looked at Alex, then looked back at the Top Banana again. "I *knew* there was a second half-drowned rat on this floating junkheap somewhere – I *felt* it. What's Big Jim doing here?"

"Big Jim?" Alex said.

"You think my mother named me Top Banana? What kind of mother would do a thing like that?"

Big Jim. Alex looked to Freda for an explanation but she was looking up at the Top Banana as if she'd just discovered something that delighted her. "Let me guess – you were down on your hands and knees behind the door because you dropped your contact lenses – am I right? You look like an old dead sea lion I saw washed up on the beach once. Somebody needs to grab you at both ends and wring you *out.*"

The Top Banana did not look embarrassed to be talked to· like this. In fact, he looked rather pleased. "I was down there praying that someone beautiful and kind would come along to rescue us."

Freda snorted. "Well, maybe you better give 'er another try, I'm not feeling very kind. Brilliant maybe. And wearing a brand-new, beautiful pair of boots."

The boots looked exactly the same as her other boots. Big and yellow. Her skinny legs grew up from inside them like mop handles sticking out of buckets.

The Top Banana looked at Alex as though he had just thought of something. "This uncle," he said. Then he stopped, apparently making a great effort to think about something. "So Alex is now the second person his bad temper has driven out of that town."

Then his face lit up. "If he's your uncle, that means you must be – !" He stopped and studied Alex's face, then turned to Freda. "This is Larry McGuire's boy?"

"Bingo!" Freda said. "Brilliant deduction! Give the man a teddy bear."

Big Jim Bryant? Alex looked hard at the man and tried to remember. "Were you the one my dad told me stories about? Like the time he helped you hide the teacher's car?"

The Top Banana grinned. "He ever tell you about the time he and Big Jim Bryant tied up the boss on a summer job?"

Yes! Again and again he'd heard Dad tell about their growing up together! "Used toilet paper to do it?"

"I think I saw that fellow's picture years later in a magazine – treasures of ancient Egypt!"

"And once you dived in to save my dad's life."

"Lost my bathing suit too. Rescued him, but had to stay under water until someone brought my pants."

"Too bad," Freda said. "Think of all the trouble we'd be saved if they'd left you there. But let's go. There's a fortune in seaweed waiting."

"Maybe we'll get a reward for bringing them in," Felicity said, "like convicts."

The Top Banana refused to go anywhere. He wasn't going to abandon his palace just like that, he said, not even if there was only half of it left. "You go on back to town. I'll just drift with my floating castle until we bump into another spot where we can tie up and call it home."

"But what if – " Alex said, but changed his mind. "I'm not going back either then, unless you go too. Let's both go hitch-hiking east. I bet you'd like it there." They could both stay with Mark. All three of them could skate on the canal, or go cross-country skiing in Gatineau Park. Alex even knew where they could find skates big enough for those feet.

The Top Banana – Big Jim Bryant – made it clear he would not like it there at all. "I can't skate. I faint at the sight of snow. Forget it."

Scornfully Felicity said, "And you're *both* just scared to come on back to town!"

Big Jim Bryant looked at Freda but she'd gone to the doorway and stood sniffing the air. He looked at Felicity. Then he looked at Alex. But he said this in the direction of Frantic Freda's back. "I guess the worst they could do is chase me out again. But what if they still believe your uncle's lies?"

Alex couldn't help saying this. "What if, what if, what if!"

"Okay!" Laughing, the Top Banana held up an arm to protect himself from attack. "Serves me right." He shook his head from side to side and turned to hold onto a windowsill while he looked out. "The biggest mischief-maker in the world – our own imagination."

"So ditch yours," Felicity said. "Get real for a change and let's get off this thing you call your 'palace' – it's really a shack that's heading for bottom, okay?"

The Top Banana looked at Felicity. "The greatest mischief-maker but also the greatest idea-maker, if you can tell the difference." He waved a hand towards Alex's wall paintings. "Look how those cartoons make you want to smile!" He indicated his own bathtub. "Look at the champion racer! A brilliant design, practically a work of genius – and I thought of it myself!" He shook his head slowly from side to side, trying to understand something. "Cartoons and racing bathtubs start with *What if*'s too – but not the kind of *What if*'s that scares the daylight out of us." Then he started to laugh for getting so carried away. "A design for an intergalactic space ship right now could get us *all* out of this mess!" Then abruptly he stopped laughing and frowned at Felicity. "Why do you keep your hand over your mouth? Somebody knock out a tooth?"

Felicity shook her head.

"Then you must be chewing on something so good you know we'd want to share it if we saw."

Felicity looked down. Then suddenly she sucked in her breath so hard that her chest swelled out; she turned up her face again so that they could see her freckles, pulled her hand away from her lips and opened her mouth wide to show off two rows of railroad tracks across her teeth.

"Braces!" Alex said. Why hadn't he noticed before? Brand-new braces, just like his.

"Oh, dear," said the Top Banana. "So they've harnessed you too. Let's see." He leaned down and squinted hard for a good look. "Another cage to keep the little white birds from flying out. And they look as if they're in there to stay a while."

Freda explained. "Her parents took her to the orthodontist months ago to get them made. Yesterday he stuck them in. Otherwise he's quite a decent man."

"Merry Christmas!" Felicity said. "I feel like putting my head in a paper bag for the next two years and never talking to *anyone!*"

So this was why she'd been watching him so closely the last while. This was why she'd said things – to see how he handled what he had to put up with. To prepare herself.

"Everybody, duck!" cried Frantic Freda. "A boat!"

All four of them crouched down out of sight in a dry corner. Maybe the boat would go right past.

But someone cut the motor, and the boat could be heard drifting close.

"Anybody in there?"

Uncle's voice.

"Anybody alive?"

"If they were dead, do you think they'd answer?" Aunt said. "Pull up so we can go in for a look."

Alex peered through a crack in the wall. The boat moved around the shack. "Anybody inside?" Uncle's voice. "We're looking for a – we're trying to find a little kid that was kidnapped."

"You going to tell your entire history to a drowning

shack?" said Aunt. "Pull over, I'll climb inside myself. Maybe he's unconscious."

Freda looked at Alex and crossed her eyes while she wobbled her head. He felt too tense even to think of laughing.

The Top Banana wrapped his arms around his knees and put his face down. He was breathing hard.

The boat drifted around the corner and bumped against the shack.

"What if they see your boat?" Alex whispered.

"I hear something," Uncle said.

"Look! A boat!"

Now both their voices were going at once. Whose was it? What did it mean? Now they were sure there was someone inside – but who?

"Dangerous criminals?"

"I shoulda brought my shotgun."

"Oh, sure. You don't know one end of the gun from another, you'd finish us both off and save the criminals the trouble."

"Would not! What do you know about anything?"

"Pull in," Aunt said. "I'm going inside."

"Oh no, you're not, you mudshark," said Frantic Freda, snatching the cap off Alex's head and hurrying to the tilted door.

"I was so sure I would find that long-legged little beggar in here," she called. "An empty shack!" She stood on the lip of the raft. "What are we gonna do?" She held up Alex's SMILE cap and heaved a great sob.

"Where did you find that?" Uncle yelled.

Aunt screeched, "Floating?"

Freda let out a heartbroken wail. What an actress!

"Floating," Aunt answered herself.

Alex watched her through a crack between the boards.

She put both hands to her face and whirled on Uncle Grump. "Now see what you've done! What are we going to tell his father? What'll people say when they hear he's drowned?"

Freda sat down on the planks and hung her head. "There's only one hope your kid could still be alive."

"You said he was *drowned!*" Aunt shouted. "This lunatic doesn't know what she's talking about."

"You'd better hustle your butts, though. I have this *feeling* . . . he's in the cookhouse!"

Silence. Alex closed his eyes and thought: Go.

Then Aunt's voice, "I think you're hiding him in there, you old bat. Trying to make fools of us."

Alex's stomach hurt. He'd be plucked out of here like a garden weed and tossed into that boat and taken home where they would ruin his life and somehow find a way to call it Natural Consequences.

"Stand aside, Freda," the Top Banana said. He pressed both hands on his knees and stood up. Then he started towards the door.

"They'll catch you!" Alex warned.

The Top Banana hooked his thumbs together in front of him, ducked his head, and dived into the water. As soon as his head came to the surface, he started to swim. Aunt screamed, "Who's that?" The Top Banana set out with the long strong strokes of an experienced swimmer. Face down, turned to one side, gulping air, face down again. Stroke. Stroke. Heading towards the shore.

Aunt and Uncle's boat set off after the swimmer. Both of them were yelling now, "Who is it? Who is it? Is it him? Stop! Stop!"

"That man is still scared of your uncle after all these years," Freda said. She looked at Alex. "How about you?" She seemed eager to have an adventure. "You gonna sit on your backside or what?"

There was only one thing to do. "Quick!" Alex jumped into Felicity's boat. Pushed at buttons, turned levers, pushed again. Eventually the motor started.

"What are you doing?" Felicity screeched. "Are you crazy?" But she was in the boat with him, untying the rope. Freda had one leg in, one out. She would split in two like a wishbone. Felicity grabbed her hand and hauled her in.

"Ram them," Freda ordered. She was the Admiral again. "C'mon."

Felicity screamed at that. "*Ram* them? You want splintered boats and bodies all over the place?" She was trying to take over the controls but Alex kept himself in her way. "Hey-e-e-ee-e-e-e-e-ey!" she yelled.

Freda held on, her eyes clamped tight and her mouth screwed up into a tiny O. She was enjoying this.

Aunt noticed him first. "There he is."

Even from this distance he could see that Uncle's face was as red as the big man's bathtub. Cursing, he swung his boat out of its circle and headed this way.

"Quick!" Freda said. Her eyes were open now. "Swing right. Lead the Bobbsey Twins away!" She was trying to stand, trying to point.

A siren!

A new boat was heading this way, much bigger than either of theirs, a pair of loudspeakers mounted on the roof.

"Cops!" Freda cried.

Alex turned the wheel again; he looked straight ahead. He wouldn't think of it now. He'd think of it later.

"Oh no, he doesn't see them," Felicity said.

"Look out!"

Not even the loud *thunk*, not even the horrible squeal of wood against metal was enough to make Alex look back.

"They didn't exactly crash," Felicity said. "It was more of a sideswipe. Nobody's hurt."

His aunt's and uncle's boat had stalled, Alex could see when he turned to glance back that way. It sat bobbing on the waves not far from the police cruiser, its nose pushed in. Uncle was standing up, hollering at the police, shaking his fist. Aunt was hollering at Uncle. At the rear of the larger boat a policeman threw a coil of rope out for them to catch.

Alex turned the steering wheel to swing the boat around and head back to the shore, where he hoped the Top Banana would be waiting – if he'd made it.

"You know how to stop this thing?" You couldn't miss the sarcasm in Felicity's voice.

At this speed they would be three city blocks into the trees before it came to a halt.

"Get out of her way!" cried Freda.

Felicity took control of the boat, while Alex concentrated on searching the shoreline for the familiar figure of Big Jim Bryant, the Top Banana. Freda was already peering through the binoculars.

"Maniacs," Felicity said, "all of them."

Trees. Trees. Trees. There were just a few small clearings along the coastline, and mossy rock cliffs occasionally slanted down to crescent beaches lined with driftwood logs. But mostly there were just thousands of trees, all green, green, green, and dripping.

But there he was, sitting on a log, resting his chin on his hands, his elbows on his knees, watching them approach. Alex and Felicity got out and hurried up the slope to him.

"Well, at least this time I didn't lose my pants."

"This time you weren't rescuing anyone either," Alex said. "You were running away."

"Running away! Running away! Easy to see you've lived all your life in a city. Haven't you ever scared up a mother grouse?"

Alex had never even seen a grouse. He wasn't sure he knew what a grouse was – some kind of bird.

"Diversionary tactics!" Freda exclaimed from the boat. She clapped her hands, delighted. "You mean you were leading them away from *us*?"

Alex laughed. "We were leading them away from *you*!"

The Top Banana ran a big hand over the bald front half of his head and laughed.

Freda climbed over the side of the boat and came sloshing up the beach. With fists on her hips, she looked them over. "You can park yourselves at my place for a while, I guess. Until feelings cool down."

"Not me," Felicity said. "I'm not scared to go home."

"Did you ask your old man if you could borrow his boat?" Freda asked. She sniffed the air, then bent over and stuck a finger into the water near her feet. She licked the finger. "Another big change coming. Proceed with caution!"

Felicity looked out across the inlet to where the police were still trying to do something about the uncle's boat. "Not everybody's lucky enough to be picked on by adults as easy to fool as those two."

When they'd all got into the boat and Alex was using the oar to push them out to where the water was deep enough to start the motor, Felicity added, "On second thought, I guess *all* adults are that easy to fool when they let themselves get so mad they're out of control."

The Top Banana looked at Alex and wriggled his eyebrows. "Just think what she's going to be like when she's older!" He shuddered all over at the thought.

Felicity grinned. "Sometimes I wonder why people don't just let me run the world myself. Things would be a lot easier if they gave me total control."

"Let's go!" Freda called. She scooped Alex's cap up from the bottom of the boat and slapped it on his head. SMILE. Then she turned to Big Jim Bryant and gave him a friendly punch on the arm. "First I chase you away," she said, "then I bring you back. Some of them will be a little surprised."

"No more surprised than I am myself," the big man said, "but I'm too worn out to resist."

Chapter Eight

Once they'd reached Freda's seaweed factory in the sunken boat at the end of the breakwater, she wouldn't even let them go outdoors in case they were seen from shore. "Just wait till things cool down."

Through the smeared window Alex could see the people of the town rushing about, trying to clean up the mess left behind by the storm. Bulldozers moved down the streets, pushing piles of limbs and roots and mud ahead of them to make giant heaps on the beach. Firemen rode their snorkels up into the air to rescue pets and chairs and bicycles off the roofs of houses. Through Freda's binoculars Alex watched a family coax an old man in pajamas down off the peak of the church roof where he wrapped one arm around the chimney and would not let go of the big stuffed teddy bear he kept under his arm. How had he got up there?

Trucks roared back and forth, hauling debris. People shovelled mud out of their doorways and raked seaweed from their walls and hosed sea water off their windows. Mr. Hamilton stood in his front yard and looked over his rust-coloured hedge, which had been torn right out by the roots and left scattered all over the road. Mrs. Pike struggled to prop up the sagging verandah roof at the front of his aunt's store. The post slipped and the roof gave her a bop on the head, so she went inside and slammed the door behind her.

Why hadn't they just told Freda, "Thank you very much for coming to rescue us," then walked the length of the breakwater in to town and gone home? It wasn't hard for Alex to understand why. After taking a good look out that window at all the activity, no one felt ready yet. Felicity turned away and said, "You were right – my old man's gonna be furious about his boat."

Big Jim Bryant sucked in a great shuddering breath, like someone about to go out on stage before an unfriendly audience, then wrung his hands together. "It'll be a shock when they see me – as if the storm isn't enough."

Alex couldn't find his aunt and uncle in the crowd, but he could imagine the mood they must be in. "Those two will *hate* it that someone else saved my life," he said.

Felicity poked Alex. "They'll probably send you to one of those private schools where they flog you if you don't get A's."

Freda looked pleased. "No rush, kids. Give that stirred-up bunch of cranky mudsharks time to cool down a bit."

"The Duchess-in-exile's shed doesn't look damaged," Alex said, "but I should go check on something I left inside."

Freda had changed into a great loose pair of men's work jeans with red elastic braces, and a torn yellow slicker, and the part of the matching hat that was still attached to the brim. Somehow she'd convinced them to help her out with her work. "A chance to demonstrate your boundless gratitude." How could they refuse? Since the tide was far out, she took Alex down onto the ocean floor on the side of the boat that couldn't be seen from town, so he could scoop up the abandoned seaweed off the wrinkled sand. In this shallow bay when the tide was out, the edge of the water was so far away you could imagine the entire ocean had dried up.

Alex pinched his nose. Seaweed was not his favourite smell.

He was not the only one put to work, of course. Freda handed Felicity a barn fork and told her, "Go scoop up seaweed into the dryers." Felicity made a face. Then Freda sent Big Jim Bryant out onto the deck. "Hose down the seaweed that Alex delivers – get rid of the salt." Big Jim eyed the large black rubber hose in his hands, then looked at Alex as if to ask: What am I doing here?

"A bustling factory here!" Freda sang out. "All of us happy as pigs in muck." It seemed to Alex that she was the only one who was happy.

Before Felicity went downstairs to Freda's dryers, she glared over the railing, her brow lowered in a terrible scowl. "Whaddaya think we are – your slaves?"

But Freda continued to look cheerful. "We don't need *them* when we've got ourselves!"

When the wheelbarrow was heaped up to the point of almost tipping over, Alex had to push it up the ramp of old planks and onto the deck of Freda's boat, for Big Jim Bryant to hose. Big Jim winked. "Tell me when your arms are about to fall off. We can trade jobs. I know you're jealous of me, washing the ocean clean of salt!"

When Alex crouched on his heels for a rest, Freda's voice rang out, "Time for sitting around on your backsides later! When that tide comes in, most of this stuff is gonna get washed away. Think of the profits I'll lose!"

Working for Aunt and Uncle on the log boom hadn't been as hard as this. Alex began to think: Since I'm going to have to go back to their place sooner or later anyway, why am I doing this? "I guess I'd better go home," he eventually said. "What if they're really worried?"

Freda straightened her back. At first she looked as though she could not believe what she'd heard. Then, perhaps because she could see he was serious, she looked hurt. "Where would you be right now if I hadn't come along when I did? Giving a case of indigestion to a whale maybe. Riding a log to the South Pacific if you were lucky. Or ducking punches from those crazy yahoo relatives of yours!"

It was easier to keep on forking up the seaweed into the wheelbarrow than to tell an offended Freda how he felt.

When she finally took them inside for tea and cookies, Alex wondered if she felt sorry for the way she'd been acting. At any rate, it was a chance for them all to rest.

Fishing nets were draped across the walls, with wooden floats and oyster shells and dried starfish caught in the folds. Also twisted pieces of driftwood with painted-on eyes, and the shell bodies of large crabs, and the stuffed carcasses of resentful-looking fish.

When they were all sitting – on boxes and three-legged chairs – Freda said, "Of course I can't force you to stay, but I'd think twice before going across to that pack of stirred-up barracudas in town. If there's one thing people hate more than a storm that wrecks everything, it's putting in a night worrying about kids that are lost."

Felicity pulled her mouth into a tight angry line. "Someone go get Lincoln. He freed the slaves in his own country but forgot about us. I guess she's gonna put us in chains next."

Big Jim Bryant leaned over and peered into the eyes of a furious big dogfish caught in the nets. "This old fellow knows what Freda's up to, don't you, pal?" He put a finger on the tip of the fish's snout. "She's just waiting until we drop so she can have us stuffed and add us to her collection." He rolled his widened eyes around to look into Felicity's eyes, and then into Alex's. Alex could see he was trying hard not to roar out with laughter.

When Big Jim Bryant finally laughed out loud, Alex couldn't help but do the same. Even Felicity Bogg had to smile, though it looked as though it hurt.

Freda didn't laugh. She jumped up and opened a cupboard door and found a great round chocolate cake which she placed in the middle of the table. "I don't suppose you like chocolate cake with gooey icing, but you can help yourself if you want – take big pieces." She watched while they cut themselves wedges of cake. "I'll tell you what! Soft-hearted lame-brained fool that I am, I'm prepared to make partners of you all. You'll make yourselves a fortune if you work with me."

While Freda had her back turned to the table, looking through a drawer for a knife, Felicity scribbled something on a scrap of paper. She slipped it under the table and nudged Alex's leg. On the front it said "Duchezz," and inside, "Help!" When he looked at Felicity, she just opened her eyes wide as though to say, Well, *do* it!

"One day," Freda said, "we'll be partners in the

biggest golldarned factory on this rainy coast. I'll give you ten percent of the company each – whaddaya say to that?"

"But – !" Alex nearly shouted this, he could hardly help himself. "What happens to the other seventy percent?"

Freda flashed Alex a look that said: Why is there always a smart-mouth kid around to spoil things? "Fifteen, then."

"Twenty-five percent each would make us equal partners," Felicity said. Her knee nudged Alex's leg again. She pulled another face. There was something he should be doing. He knew what it was.

Freda sat down and pressed her fork onto the crumbs around the edges of her plate until she had gathered them all, then she raised the fork to her mouth. "You gotta admit, with all my other talents I'm one heck of a terrific cook!"

"Are you trying to bribe us?" Big Jim asked.

"Haven't you heard?" Freda said, chewing her cake. "I'm supposed to be jaybird crazy. Any of those land-locked predators over there could tell you that."

"I don't believe it." Big Jim pushed his chair back and folded his arms. "You're no more crazy than I am."

"Exactly what I was thinking," Felicity said. "Which is why I'm getting out of here. Coming, Alex?" But she was already out the door. Through the window Alex could see her running along the breakwater towards town, yelling, "Hey-e-e-e-e-e-ey!"

"What if she brings the army?" Alex said.

Big Jim Bryant and Freda looked at one another. Big Jim snorted first. "The army?" he said. Then Freda laughed. Big Jim laughed louder. Freda started shaking all over and hauled a red-and-white handkerchief out of her overalls to wipe at her eyes.

"You're laughing at me," Alex said.

But this only started them laughing again. Alex was just about to step out the door and follow Felicity in to town when Big Jim Bryant finally got enough control of himself to say, "We weren't laughing at you, we were laughing at ourselves."

Freda said, "The army swooped down on us once."

"When Freda and I caused a public disturbance," Big Jim said.

"After he'd won a bathtub race."

"And we were celebrating."

"After everyone else had finished celebrating."

"We made too much noise."

"Dancing on people's roofs!" Freda cried out. "We swore we would dance until dawn. When the police didn't answer someone's complaint – worn out themselves from celebrating – they called in the army. Said they'd been invaded by a pair of aliens!"

"I bet I know something," Big Jim said to Freda when they had both got over their laughing fit. His voice had softened, his smile was kind. "I bet you thought if you let us go we'd never come back to visit."

Freda's face went serious. She shrugged and started devouring the chocolate cake. It was true that no one ever came out to visit Freda. Even Alex just visited for a few moments out on the end of the wharf when he delivered the shells he'd collected for her jewelry.

"Yoo hoo!" The gangplank bounced noisily as someone crossed from the giant boulders of the breakwater to the deck of the ship. Whoever this was tapped gently at the door.

"Whaddaya want?" Freda called. She poked at the gooey icing on her cake and did not get up from her chair.

110

"Freda? It's me . . . " Alex recognized the Duchess-in-exile's voice. "I feel rather foolish talking to a rusty door."

Freda made a face to imitate the snooty face of someone who talked so polite. "I'm not home. Just leave your calling card."

"Why don't you let her in?" Alex said.

"You let her in if you're so crazy about her." Freda scowled down at her plate.

"Freda?" said the Top Banana, looking surprised. He went to the door himself and opened it.

When the Duchess-in-exile came inside, Big Jim Bryant's face turned red all the way up across the high bald forehead to his hair; his grin spread out from ear to ear. Alex remembered him saying: "Like a mother to me. My best audience."

"Freda!" the Duchess-in-exile said. "What could you have been *thinking!* Keeping him all to yourself!" On her shoulder Mrs. Digby-Smith yawned widely, already bored.

Freda pushed a wedge of cake towards her latest visitor.

"Oh no, I couldn't," said the Duchess-in-exile, who seemed to have eyes for no one but Big Jim Bryant. She barely glanced at Freda, and hadn't even noticed yet that Alex was here.

"Park yourself," Freda demanded, pouring a cup of tea. "Drink this."

Mrs. Digby-Smith's ears perked up when she saw the dead animals in the fishing nets, but the Duchess-in-exile looked at them as though she couldn't be certain she was safe here. "I've more cleaning up of my own to do. There's sea water and mud in my bathtub, and something big stuck in my chimney – maybe a porpoise? I've got to get it out. I don't know if anyone's going to have the strength for tonight's party." She looked at Big Jim Bryant. Mrs. Digby-Smith stared into the eyes of the biggest captive fish.

"What party?" Alex said. He couldn't imagine anyone in this town going to a party, except perhaps to spoil it.

The Duchess-in-exile didn't seem surprised to see Alex here. "It's an annual event. A Christmas Eve get-together." She sipped at her tea, thought a moment and sipped again. "You make a good cup of tea, Freda. Why didn't I know that before?"

"You've never come to visit me before," Freda said.

"The comic books aren't wet?" Alex asked.

The Duchess-in-exile shook her head. "Not a drop. I checked."

Alex was relieved to hear it. "When we go over to the party, I'll come by and have a look for myself." He glanced at scowling Freda. It was time to take a stance. "*I'm* going. Aren't you?"

"Oh, no one's allowed to stay away from this!" the Duchess-in-exile declared. "Once a year everybody makes this attempt to be nice to one another. They can't remember why they try, but still they wouldn't think of cancelling it. It will be just the right time for you to make your return!" She put a hand on Big Jim's arm. "And you too. Tonight of all nights they would never chase you out of town."

Meowing loudly, Mrs. Digby-Smith suddenly leapt off the Duchess-in-exile's shoulder and onto the back of the biggest captive dogfish. Was she hungry? Together, she and the petrified fish rocked back and forth from the force of the jump, shaking starfish and green-glass fishermen's floats out of the net. Then cat and fish also fell out of the net and dropped to the floor – the cat on its feet, the fish on its nose. The fish stayed where it fell, stiff as a slab of lumber, but the cat went yowling out through the window above the sink and streaked back to town.

Chapter Nine

By the time the story had been told – to Aunt and Uncle, to the police and members of the rescue squad – Uncle didn't have the energy left to be as angry as he wanted to be.

"Go hang around Big Jim Bryant," he said. "Your father never had time for me either, when we were kids. Big Jim was always more fun. I had to listen to 'Big Jim this' and 'Big Jim that' right through my whole blinkin' childhood. You might as well do the same. I'm going to bed."

Aunt wasn't going to bed early like Uncle, but she would not go to the party either. "You better go show your face, though," she told Alex. "Otherwise they'll be saying even worse things about us behind our backs."

When Alex stepped inside the old community hall, he saw that Big Jim and Freda hadn't yet arrived, but Miss MacAdam and Mrs. Blimmer were wrangling over table decorations, while Mr. O'Reilly and Mr. Bond bickered about the seating arrangements. Billie Tonelli was down on the floor wrestling with Jake Marinus, but he suddenly leapt up to spray artificial snow in Felicity's hair. She swung her arm back and drove a fist into his chest, knocking him to the floor.

Someone had hung a few Christmas decorations, but

the big old hall was still pretty bare – great high walls made from sheets of plywood painted a pale uninteresting green. Gymnastic ropes hung from the ceiling beams. Vaulting horses and parallel bars had been pushed into a corner. A coloured photograph of the Queen hung over the doors that said *Ladies* and *Gents.* People sat in tight circles of identical wooden chairs and raised their voices into one another's face. Alex decided to stay close to the door and wait for Big Jim.

Felicity came over, pulling a disgusted face. She gathered up all her hair in her hands and wiped off the artificial snow. "Yuk." Alex hauled a handkerchief out of the clean pants he'd put on before coming, and she used it to clean her hands. "Waiting for those loonies to get here?"

When Mr. O'Reilly and Mr. Bond got into a wrangle over the seating arrangements, the Duchess-in-exile stood up in her bright-blue gown and sparkling jewels and clanked a spoon against a glass. She looked down at the crowd with such majesty and disapproval that everyone grew silent. Mrs. Digby-Smith was asleep on her shoulder – worn out, perhaps, from her tussle with the dead fish.

"Have you ever stopped to listen to yourselves?"

No one moved. "Instead of fighting," the Duchess-in-exile said, "should we not be celebrating? After all, look who's come back today!"

Everyone looked towards the door, but their eyes were not on Alex. The Top Banana was standing in the doorway, with Frantic Freda wedged in at his side.

"Big Jim!" somebody yelled.

"*Aaaaaaaaaaaaaaa!*" Miss MacAdam threw up her hands and screeched with surprise. Others dropped their jaws open – they couldn't believe what they saw. Would they be angry? What if they chased the Top Banana out of town?

But everyone broke into laughter. The Top Banana was doing a little dance for them, kicking out one foot and then the other, tipping an imaginary hat. Then he put up his arms and threw himself down to stand on his hands. He did a back flip, then another, until he'd back-flipped right across the room to stand by the Duchess-in-exile, who gave him her jewelled hand to kiss.

"I guess you folks are a little surprised to see me," the Top Banana said in a great loud voice. "I'm a little surprised myself."

"We thought they musta put you in jail!" someone shouted.

"Well, they didn't put me in jail, but I haven't been idle either," said Big Jim. "I've dreamed up ways of breaking the sound barrier with my bathtub. I'm going to be your Champion again – just wait."

While everyone applauded, he started to undo the straps of his overalls. He unbuttoned his shirt. He dropped his overalls and stepped out of them. Loud cheering was added to the applause. There stood the Top Banana in a skin-tight silvery uniform with a huge yellow banana on his chest and a wide crimson cape falling from his shoulders. He whipped a black mask out of a pocket and strapped it over his eyes.

"I rooted around in the storeroom back there to see if you'd thrown it away," he said. "I'm ready."

Alex moved closer to have a good look at his costume.

Great guffaws came from the crowd. "I didn't realize how much I missed that man," someone said.

"*Hoo-ee!*" someone else yelled.

"*Hoo-ee!*" the Top Banana yelled back. Then he

turned to Alex. "All my life I wanted to be a comic book hero. I had the greatest collection west of the Rockies. I had them all. Still have them too" – he lowered his voice – "stored in the Duchess-in-exile's boathouse, though she doesn't know it. Then I decided: Why should the guys in those comics have all the fun? That's when I got into bathtub racing." He jumped onto the table, placed his feet on either side of a platter heaped with turkey, and grabbed at the gymnast rope which hung from the ceiling beams. Then he swung out over the floor like Tarzan, his feet kicking out unpredictably this way and that, causing people to duck if they did not want to be knocked down. Laughing, he swooped up at the far end and stood on the piano. From the top of the piano he launched out again, and came swooping back across the crowd to land beside Alex.

"Back in my shack, when I asked you to do my portrait, you wouldn't do it," the Top Banana said. "How about now?"

"But – " Alex looked at the crowd, who were all looking at them as if they were thinking: Why would our Champion bother with that long-legged trouble-maker from Back East? "Whaddaya say, folks?" the big man said. "Wouldn't you like to see just one of those boring plywood panels decorated with the Top Banana's picture? You've got the Queen over there – why not me?"

Alex wished that he hadn't come. What if – what if they decided it was time to show him how offended they'd been by his picture? What if they decided to punish him now?

But the crowd cheered. People ran to the storeroom and returned with buckets of paint. "Let the long-legged kid decorate the walls!" they shouted. It seemed the

Top Banana could make them forget anything. They insisted that Alex do the portrait right away. They sent people into the storeroom to look for cans of paint.

"Don't forget his stomach!" cried Felicity's mother. "You'll need a second wall for that!"

The Top Banana stood up on a table, posing like a weight-lifter showing off his muscles. Freda put a long bony hand against the nearest piece of wall. "This is good enough right here," she said. "Just wind 'er up and let 'er rip, boy! Show this pack of snooty crustaceans what you can do."

Alex looked at Freda. She was serious. He looked at Big Jim Bryant – once his father's best friend. He looked at Felicity, who rolled her eyes back into her head and threw out her hands in a gesture of helplessness. Was she giving up on him? He dipped the paint brush into the can, brought it up and touched it to the wall. The room was silent. Waiting, he guessed, to see if he was going to be mean – as they believed that trouble-making picture had been mean. He stood up on a bench so that he could reach high enough, then drew a long curved thick vertical line to get things started. Now it was impossible not to go ahead.

When he'd sketched in the high bald forehead and put eyes on the Top Banana's face, he heard murmurs throughout the room, as though everyone had been holding his breath.

When he'd drawn the big man's stomach, with the huge banana on his chest, everyone clapped. He still felt nervous, but he had to admit he liked seeing all those friendly faces enjoying themselves. He frowned and leaned close. Arms. Hands. The cape. The bathtub – he was standing up in his bathtub with the wind blowing both the ostrich tail and his cape out behind. Big smiling mouth. Teeth. An armload of trophies. When it seemed he might be finished, Alex stepped back to look it over. Not bad. But it needed a little shading here and there, to give it some bulk, a bit of depth. He worked quickly, but did not put his initials on the side of the tub until he was sure it was finished and right. He didn't know what else to do but turn to his audience and bow.

People clapped and whistled as the Top Banana got down from the table and shook Alex's hand. "The Queen is turning green with envy over there."

While the Top Banana was admiring Alex's drawing, Frantic Freda removed the food from the table, then climbed up onto it and sat on a chair facing the crowd, still wearing her yellow boots and her torn yellow hat. "My turn," she said. She looked at Alex to explain: "It's a tradition around here. Everyone takes a turn entertaining before we dig into the food."

She announced that she would imitate famous voices. "First, Barbra Streisand," she said, before singing a few bars in a high squawking voice. People put their hands over their ears and rolled their eyes. Then, "Prime Minister Thatcher of Britain." But Mrs. Thatcher sounded exactly the same as Barbra Streisand, and so did Robert Redford. Still, everyone cheered happily after each one.

What if he did a comic portrait of her too?

The idea, when it popped into his head, shocked Alex. Where had it come from?

He looked at Freda, having such a good time doing such a bad job. What if Freda were not Freda? What would she be? A seagull. Or some other scrawny long-beaked seabird found scurrying this way and that all over the beach.

While she squawked her way through imitations of Jane Fonda and Kermit the Frog, Alex took up his paint brush and drew her as a scrawny seagull ventriloquist wearing a tuxedo made from seaweed, with wooden dummies sitting on her lap, all of them seabirds just exactly like her.

When Freda saw what he'd done, she stopped her act and studied the picture. Alex held his breath, felt his heart beating. "At least seagulls keep the beach clean for you landlubbers," she said. Then she laughed. So did everyone else. She made the high shrieking sound of an excited seagull which has spotted some tasty garbage, and everyone laughed again. Then she climbed down off the table and went through the crowd, oaring her high elbows like a seagull's wings, and passed out pieces of her seashell jewelry from a gunnysack. "Tourists aren't breaking their necks to buy them, that's for sure," she said. "Somebody might as well have them. Merry Christmas!" People looked at the periwinkle brooches and limpet earrings in their hands. "Now put them *on!*"

Beneath the photograph of the Queen, the slow and half-awake Mr. Klinck sat down to play the piano, though he had difficulty finding some of the keys – a few had been stolen. The fact that the piano was also badly out of tune did not seem to discourage him. Chubby Mrs. Lever ducked into the *Ladies*, then came out in an ancient ballerina costume and skittered across the floor. While Mr. Klinck plonked away, hunched over the yellowed, incomplete keyboard, she turned several circles on her toes, swung her arms through the air like broken helicopter blades, and tripped over her own feet.

What if he painted her too? And Mr. Klinck? This idea surprised Alex even more than the idea of doing Frantic Freda. Freda was a friend but these two were strangers –

unpredictable, maybe even dangerous.

Alex looked at the long grey solemn face of Mr. Klinck at the piano. Mr. Klinck looked back at Alex from under his half-closed eyelids. His fingers kept on plunking away. What if he got furious at being turned into a cartoon? What if he threw a fit – lifted the piano up off the floor in a superhuman rage and threw it? But Mr. Klinck raised one eyebrow just a little, and just barely smiled. Maybe he knew exactly what Alex was thinking.

What if Mr. Klinck believed that he had as much right to be painted onto the community wall as the Top Banana had, or Frantic Freda?

So Mr. Klinck became a great blue heron, long and skinny and shaped like a question mark, hunched over the piano keyboard waiting for a fish to swim by. Alex felt nervous while he worked, expecting a great hand to clamp down on his shoulder from behind, waiting for someone to yell: "What does that brat think he's doing?" But no one protested, and the great blue heron took shape. Far too serious, much too skinny, but wonderfully patient. And just as quickly, Mrs. Lever became a swan trying to dance with huge running shoes on her feet – a ridiculous figure but brave.

Silence. Everyone, including the two performers, looked at the drawing. Then they looked at one another. They looked at Alex. What were they thinking? What were they going to do?

Mr. Klinck's long grey face grew even longer. Then it twitched. Then it almost smiled. Mr. Klinck hiccoughed, and trembled, and finally exploded into a laugh. This broke the silence and everyone laughed – laughed and applauded.

Now others were coming forward to entertain the

crowd, all of them grinning at the pictures. What if he did them all? Were they in a good mood just because they were at a party, or because they were relieved they'd survived the storm – or had something really changed? "What if I decorated the wall with cartoons of them all?"

Miss MacAdam juggled three red balls and became a trained seal wearing a giant red wig. This took more courage than anything else so far. Alex broke into a sweat while he worked, but Miss MacAdam responded by turning her wig around backwards and juggling the balls even higher. Piston-rod Joe, who demonstrated how to change a flat tire in a rain storm, became a giant wrench. Mr. Hamilton recited the famous poem that began, "I think that I shall never see a poem lovely as a tree," something he said he'd learned years ago when he went to school with Big Jim Bryant and Alex's dad. What if Mr. Hamilton were not a man? He would be a tree, of course. Remembering that Mr. Hamilton had been the one to give him a ride on his way to check up on his seedlings, Alex drew him as a giant Douglas fir wearing thick dark-rimmed glasses and holding dozens of little firs in his branches to protect them from the dogs that waited around his feet with their legs lifted.

Alex would tell his dad about these pictures tomorrow. He was bound to call on Christmas Day if he was anywhere near a phone. Would Dad be able to explain why people who'd been so mad at him just days before were now lining up for a chance to let him draw their pictures on the plywood wall?

When Felicity stood up to take her turn, she sang into an imaginary microphone like a New Wave rock star. She wriggled her knees, she hopped on one foot, she threw back her head and howled. Alex was not too sure how far he should go with this one. "What kind of mood are you in?" She didn't answer; she eyed him with a steely eye while he made up his mind. "Oh well, why not live dangerously?" He drew her as a buck-toothed, long-necked chicken with a head of messy hair, squawking into an ear of corn that looked like a microphone.

"Uh-oh," somebody said. "This time he's gone too far."

"Looking for trouble," someone else said.

Felicity studied the cartoon figure. What if she decided to drive a fist into his stomach? She looked as if she might be considering it.

But her big wide braces flashed a smile. "For a dumb kid," she said to Alex, "you're not so dumb. Can I take that home with me?"

"What a nice thing it must be," Alex heard someone say, "to be able to make people smile. That kid from Back East's not so bad."

"Well, he brought the Top Banana back anyway. Who would ever have guessed how glad we are about that!"

"That old seagull Freda! I never thought of her that way myself, but now – well, that's what she is!"

"You can tell he thinks she's a funny old bat, all right, but look – he sees something else in her too. Can you imagine this place without her?"

A short distance away through the crowd, the Top Banana was grinning at Alex. Alex discovered that he was grinning himself – one of those great wide smiles that just couldn't be helped. Who would have guessed that *what if*'s could lead to this!

Again the Duchess-in-exile stood up and faced the crowd. Was she going to take her turn next? Alex wondered what kind of cartoon he could make of her.

124

A flower with a long, long stem? A runaway hiding with the stolen crown jewels in a truckload of turnips? But she was not about to entertain – not yet. She announced an intermission. "We'll break for a few Christmas carols, ladies and gentlemen. Mr. Heron-Klinck? If you don't mind seeing what musical fish swim by on that keyboard this time. Some of us will get our pictures done later."

For a short while Alex enjoyed the storm of laughter and compliments that fell upon him. He was not even sorry to see that Uncle and Aunt, unable to keep their vow to stay away from a party, had entered the hall at the far end, though of course they felt they must scowl and try to look fierce and displeased while people showed them his wall drawings. They could not spoil anything now! But soon he found an empty bench in a quiet corner and looked out at the rain, streaking down through the panels of light which the windows threw against the trees. The Top Banana came over to stand beside him. "You gonna let me see your collection tomorrow?"

"I keep my comics in plastic bags," Alex told the Top Banana. "I don't want them to fade or get marked."

"Don't worry," the big man said. "I know exactly how to turn the pages so they don't get creased."

"Tell me," Alex said, "did you ever have to wear braces on your teeth?"

"Did I? When I was your age my teeth were so crooked they had to tie them up with logging chains to straighten them out. The only nice thing about it was that while I was tied down like that, I had plenty of time for reading Superman. And Batman. And the Green Hornet. That was when I first put on a costume like this and started rescuing people in distress. At night I'd untie the chains and fly off to save whole towns from evil men, and snatch beautiful women out of the jaws of dragons."

"You telling the truth?"

Whatever the Top Banana had intended to answer was drowned out at that moment when a large group, gathered around old Mr. Klinck at the piano, broke into a loud and happy singing of a Christmas carol. A strange assortment of uncertain voices stumbled their way through the song: "Yet in thy dark streets shineth the everlasting Light / The hopes and fears of all the years are met in Thee tonight."

Felicity dropped into the chair beside Alex. "I wouldn't want to have to go saving *you* two every day! I'm pooped." She sprawled out, to demonstrate how pooped she was, then snapped into a proper sitting position again and narrowed her eyes at Alex. "If you go putting any of this in that comic book of yours, you just leave me out of it – understand?"

Alex nodded. He did not understand why she wouldn't want to be in his comic, but he definitely understood that it wouldn't be smart to go against her wishes.

Jeff Padolski, who stood alone looking in this direction, gave Alex a quick salute by tilting a finger against his forehead. Then he started ambling over.

"Unless of course you need to have someone beautiful for the love interest," Felicity said. "Then you can put me in, but only if you give me perfect teeth, like a movie star. I'm already tired of having these things in my mouth." She lifted her upper lip to show off the row of glittering braces.

Out of the corner of his eye, Alex could see that Frantic Freda was heading this way. "Just don't kiss anybody," Alex told Felicity. "You might rip off half their face."

"Just look at you!" Freda called out. "Sitting around like a bunch of worn-out old sea lions mumbling to themselves on a rock." She perched on the bench beside the Top Banana and put a hand on his silvery arm. Though she was wearing a yellow striped dress, she had not removed the torn rain hat from her explosion of electric grey hair, nor shed her new yellow boots. "I figured we'd be celebrating tonight! When does the dancing start?"

The big man grinned at Alex. "How can a fellow resist? I wonder how long it'll take them this time to call in the army to stop us."